The
CHRISTMAS
PONY

The
CHRISTMAS
PONY

MELODY CARLSON

Revell
a division of Baker Publishing Group
Grand Rapids, Michigan

© 2012 by Melody Carlson

Published by Revell
a division of Baker Publishing Group
P.O. Box 6287, Grand Rapids, MI 49516-6287
www.revellbooks.com

Printed in the United States of America

Library of Congress Cataloging-in-Publication Data
Carlson, Melody.
    The Christmas pony / Melody Carlson.
        p.   cm.
    ISBN 978-0-8007-1927-2 (cloth)
    1. Christmas stories. I. Title.
PS3553.A73257C53 2012
813'.54—dc23   2012010120

The internet addresses, email addresses, and phone numbers in this book are accurate at the time of publication. They are provided as a resource. Baker Publishing Group does not endorse them or vouch for their content or permanence.

12   13   14   15   16   17   18   7   6   5   4   3   2   1

1

December 1937

Lucy Turnbull knew better than to wish for a pony for Christmas this year. Besides receiving the upsetting news that Santa Claus was only make-believe (Tommy Farley had popped that beloved bubble several weeks ago), Lucy had been assured by Mama in no uncertain terms that she was not getting a pony—and furthermore, Lucy had no business asking for such nonsense. "You might as well ask me to buy you the moon," Mama firmly told her at the dinner table.

"Ponies are expensive," Grandma added. "Only rich people can afford those luxuries these days."

Really, Lucy should have heeded their warning. But at bedtime, after she'd finished her prayers, Lucy noticed that the corners of Mama's mouth were turned downward. Lucy pulled the covers to her chin, cringing to realize she was to blame for the two deep creases in the center of Mama's forehead. Lucy should not have asked God for a pony. Not tonight. And especially not after what Mama and Grandma had told her at dinnertime.

As Mama put an extra quilt on the bed, Lucy craned her neck, straining to see the picture she'd pinned above the metal headboard earlier. She'd drawn her dream pony on the blank side of the November calendar sheet that Grandma had nearly used as fire starter. Then, using her best penmanship, Lucy had written "Pony for Sale or Trade" across the top of her drawing—just like the sign she'd noticed this afternoon. The wooden sign had been nailed to a fence post by the Greenburg field, and Lucy knew that meant that Mr. Greenburg was selling Smoky. She'd admired the little gray pony for as long as she could remember. Seeing he was for sale had sent her running home to tell Mama and Grandma the good news.

"You know that I can barely afford to keep food on the table." Mama sighed as she leaned over to kiss Lucy's forehead. "Heaven knows I cannot afford to feed a horse as well."

"Smoky's not a horse," Lucy pointed out. "He's a pony."

"Ponies . . . horses . . . they still eat food, don't they?" Mama tucked the quilt more snugly around her. "The only extra mouths we need around here are the paying kind, Lucy. Instead of praying for a pony, why don't you ask the Good Lord to send us some boarders?"

"Yes, Mama." Lucy burrowed deeper into the covers as Mama pulled the string on the overhead light. "I *will* pray for that," she promised. Lying in the darkness, she listened as Mama's footsteps went down the hallway toward the kitchen. She heard the squeaking of the woodstove door and the clunk of a heavy piece of firewood being set inside, followed by the clanking sound of the heavy door being closed and, after a bit, the reassuring creak of the old rocker as Mama sat down.

Grandma was already in bed, but Mama always stayed up late. She was probably reaching for her knitting basket now. Lucy didn't know how it was possible, but sometimes Mama could knit a whole sock in just one single night. The socks were all made out of worsted wool, a fine black yarn that Mama said was hard on her eyes. But when Lucy suggested she use another color, a prettier one like sky blue, Mama had explained that the store would only sell her socks in black. Lucy knew that ever since Daddy died, back when she was just five, they needed Mama's socks to trade for groceries. Just like they needed paying boarders to fill the three upstairs bedrooms of the old farmhouse, because even though they earned extra money by taking in people's laundry, Lucy knew that it was never quite enough. She'd heard Mama and Grandma speak of this very thing often enough. Mostly when they didn't realize she was listening.

"We just have to make ends meet," Mama would tell Lucy sometimes, especially when Lucy couldn't have something she wanted. Usually it was something she didn't really need, like candy or toys or pretty hair ribbons. Always it was something much smaller than a pony.

Lucy was only eight years old, but she was old enough to know that times were hard. Grandma said that often enough. "Times might be hard, Lucy," she'd say in her slow, quiet way, "but you can still be thankful for what you've got—a roof over your head and food to eat." Of course, Lucy didn't think too much about those things. She was more thankful for the long rope swing over the creek, or the bird's nest she found after last week's windstorm, or getting to play an angel in this year's Christmas pageant. Those things were easy to be thankful for.

Sometimes Lucy would overhear Mama and Grandma having conversations they didn't want Lucy to be privy to, but the solemn, serious tone of their voices always made her ears perk up, and she would listen harder than ever. Like when the Saunders family lost their farm last spring and had to move away. Lucy wasn't quite sure how their neighbors "lost" their farm since, as far as she could see, it was still there. Sure, it was overgrown with blackberries and weeds and the slumping fences needed fixing, but when she walked past it on her way to school every day, it never looked lost to her. The only thing that seemed to be missing was the Saunderses themselves. Lucy missed her best friend Clara Saunders and wondered where the Saunderses' dusty green farm truck had carried Clara and her family off to and whether or not Clara was happier there.

True to her promise, Lucy closed her eyes now and, with genuine faith, prayed for God to bring them some paying boarders. Mama had just said that this time of year, with Christmas around the corner, not many travelers would be stopping in Maple Grove to stay. The best time of year for boarders always seemed to be summer. Just the same, Lucy knew that God could do anything. At least that was what Pastor McHenry liked to say. Sometimes she wasn't too sure Mama believed that exactly.

Otherwise, why would she be so worried about Lucy's prayers for a pony?

After Lucy finished praying for boarders to come and stay in the upstairs rooms, she got a brand-new prayer idea. Instead of simply asking God to give her a pony, she would ask him to give her what the pony would need to eat as well. Surely Mama wouldn't be opposed to that sort of prayer.

"And please, dear God," she said finally, "help Mama to find her smile again." Lucy could remember when Mama had the prettiest smile ever. Back when Daddy was still alive. But like Lucy's memories of her father, Mama's smile had faded some over the last few years. If Lucy couldn't have a pony for Christmas, she would settle for Mama's smile instead.

After Lucy said amen, she began to imagine what it would be like to ride Smoky to school each day. The trip to town was almost a mile, and without Clara and her sister to walk with, it had felt longer than ever this year. Lucy imagined how she'd tie her gray pony to the willow tree by the creek, close enough so he could get a cool drink to refresh himself with and where he could feed on the grass that grew lush and green there—and it occurred to her, the grass food would be free. Maybe other kinds of pony food would be free as well. She would gladly collect the mushy windfall apples for Smoky in the fall, just the ones that were too wormy for cider or anything else, although she might slip him a good one now and then too. She'd sneaked him apples before. Just the memory of the fuzzy feel of his warm muzzle on the palm of her hand made her smile, and thinking these lovely thoughts, Lucy drifted off into a sweet pony dream.

The next morning, after Lucy tended to the chickens and collected the eggs and did her other usual Saturday chores, Mama held up a small package wrapped in brown paper. Lucy knew it held this week's socks and, judging by the size, contained four pairs.

"Do you have the list ready?" Lucy pulled on her winter coat, buttoning it up to her chin. She was accustomed to doing their Saturday shopping by now. She and Grandma used to go together, but the cold, damp weather was aggravating Grandma's arthritis something fierce this year. So for the last several weeks, Lucy had been doing the Saturday errands on her own. She liked doing it herself too. Knowing Mama trusted her and that she was old enough to help out like this, well, it just felt good.

Mama handed her the sock package and a small slip of paper, and Lucy read over the list with disappointment. Only three items were on it: yeast, coffee, and baking powder. "This is *all* you need?" She tucked it into her coat pocket.

Mama shrugged. "For today, it is."

Lucy suspected that meant it was all they could afford today, but she just smiled as she pulled on her knit hat. "Well, it's not much to carry back. I guess I won't need to take my wagon."

Mama tugged the hat down over Lucy's ears. "Don't forget your mittens. It's cold out there. But at least it doesn't look like rain today. Now, be on your way and don't dillydally in town."

Lucy considered telling Mama that a pony would come in mighty handy for doing errands in town, especially on a cold day like this when she could cling to his furry coat for warmth, but she stopped herself. She might be just a kid, but she knew

10

enough to understand how that kind of talk would simply aggravate Mama. There was no sense in doing that. Even so, she would walk quickly to town and complete the errands and still have enough time to stop to visit with Smoky, and if she was lucky, maybe Mr. Greenburg would be around and she could ask him about the pony's price or inquire as to what he would consider for trade. Not that Lucy had much of anything of value to trade. But it couldn't hurt to ask. With a spring in her step, she hurried toward town.

Walking past the Saunderses' old farm, Lucy tried not to think about Clara. As she passed the Greenburg place, she waved and called out to the pony. "Hello, Smoky! I'll stop by to see you on my way home."

She was about halfway to town when she heard a car coming down the road behind her. It was making a lot of noise, and when she looked, smoke was billowing all around it. She stepped to the side of the road, watching as the pale yellow car slowly sputtered and clunked past her. Despite the cloud of smoke, it looked like a pretty car. Too bad it didn't work right.

When Lucy got to the edge of town, she noticed the pale yellow car parked in front of Hempley's Garage, and a man in a brown suit was talking to Mr. Hempley. But it was the lady getting out of the passenger side of the car who really captured Lucy's attention. Wrapped in a royal blue coat with a big silver fur collar, she had shining hair almost the same color as the pale yellow car and cut short with bangs that curled like a fringe around her pretty face.

As Lucy got closer, she could see the lady's rosy cheeks and lips of scarlet red. Lucy stopped walking, staring openly at this fancy lady. She looked just like a real movie star! Lucy had seen only a handful of motion pictures in her life, mostly the ones with Shirley Temple in them, and only during the summertime or when Mama had paying boarders and money was not so tight, but Lucy had seen enough to know that this lady looked just like the pretty actresses on the silver screen. Gripping the package of socks tightly in her arms, Lucy just stared without moving.

"Hello, doll." The lady smiled down at Lucy.

"Hello," Lucy managed to say back to her.

"Is there a place I can buy a soda around here?" Her voice sounded as sweet as sugar and honey and something else too. Maybe spice.

Lucy blinked and tried to gather her thoughts. "There's the mercantile right there." She pointed across the street. "They sell sodas in there. They have a big Coca-Cola cooler right by the front door." Then Lucy realized this lady probably meant the kind of soda that comes in a glass with a straw and ice. "But there's Ruth's Café too," she said quickly. "Down on the other end of town."

The lady hooked the handle of her shiny black handbag over her arm as she gazed across the street. "I'll be over there in the mercantile," she called out to the man in the brown suit.

"That's where I'm going too," Lucy said as she walked with the lady. "I'm doing my mama's errands today."

"Well, isn't that nice." The lady pulled her fur collar more tightly around her neck and shivered. "Brrr . . . it's cold here."

"My grandma said it might snow," Lucy said cheerfully.

"Snow?" The lady's thin eyebrows went up. "But this is Arizona. I thought it was supposed to be warm here."

"In the wintertime?" Lucy frowned.

"Oh, yes." The lady nodded as if remembering something. "George did mention the high altitude here. That probably explains it."

Lucy wasn't sure what it explained, but she couldn't think of anything else to say as they went into the store together. Even so, she watched curiously as the lady walked over to the big red cooler and selected a bottle of orange soda. Lucy knew it was impolite to stare, but she couldn't help herself as she watched this lady walking—or was she floating?—around the store, looking at the candy case and then the sundries section and finally stopping at the magazine rack.

"Hello, Lucy," Mrs. Danson called out with unusual friendliness. "Can I help you, dear?"

Lucy went over to the counter, setting her package of socks in front of Mrs. Danson. "I only need a few things today." She peeled off a mitten and reached into her coat pocket.

"Who is that with you?" Mrs. Danson whispered as she opened the package of socks, examining them closely before setting them aside.

Lucy shrugged. "I don't know."

"She's not from around here, that's for certain."

Lucy told Mrs. Danson the items on her list, and while the storekeeper went to the back room to get some yeast, the man in the brown suit came into the store. "Bad news," he told the blonde lady. "The mechanic just told me that the engine overheated."

"What does that mean?" The lady looked at him with big blue eyes.

"It means I should've stopped driving before the radiator boiled dry." He ran his hand through his short dark hair with troubled eyes. "The mechanic says he can order parts, but it will take a few days, maybe even a week, depending on how bad the damage to the engine is—and it doesn't look good."

"Oh, dear!" Her jet black eyelashes fluttered. "What on earth will we do, George? Can you get another car to get us out to California?"

He let out a big sigh, then shook his head. "I need to stick around long enough to get this car fixed."

She plunked her bottle of soda on the counter with a thud. "Do you think there's anyplace to stay in this one-horse town?"

Lucy's ears perked up now. "My mama runs a boarding house," she quickly told the lady. "We've got room."

The lady's fine brows arched. "Really?"

"It's about a mile out of town," Lucy explained. "We have three upstairs rooms and my mama is a good cook and—"

"A mile out of town?" the lady frowned.

"But it's real pretty and quiet out there," Lucy said hopefully, "and lots cheaper than the boarding house here in town." She refrained from mentioning that the place in town was said to have bedbugs since Mama would not approve. "The food is lots better at my mama's boarding house too. It's not bragging 'cause everyone says so."

"That sounds good to me." The man's brown eyes lit up.

Just like that, Lucy was explaining to them where the house was located and what color it was and that she'd run on home ahead of them and inform her mama that they were coming. "If you get there in time, you can have lunch with us too. Grandma's making chicken and dumplings today."

"I like the sound of that." The man looked at his watch and grinned. "My mouth is already starting to water."

"But a mile from town?" The lady's red lips puckered as she stuck out a shiny black shoe. "How on earth do we get there?"

The man just laughed. Meanwhile, Lucy scrambled to gather up the package that Mrs. Danson had readied for her, bidding everyone good-bye before she hurried on her way outside. Heading down the road for home, she partly walked and partly ran, but she realized that her plans for stopping by to talk to Mr. Greenburg about Smoky would have to wait for now. However, if God had already answered her prayers for paying boarders, maybe that meant he would answer her prayers for a pony as well.

2

W ho are these people?" Mama asked after Lucy had breathlessly told her the good news.

"I don't know their names," Lucy gasped as she peeled off her coat, "but they look like rich people." Now she described the yellow car and the lady's fine clothing. "I think I heard them saying they were on their way to California."

"With half of the rest of the country," Grandma said from where she was tending a pot on the stove.

"Passing through." Mama hung Lucy's coat on a peg by the door. "Everybody is just passing through Maple Grove."

"Did you get the yeast?" Grandma asked Lucy. "I'll need it to bake bread for tomorrow. Especially if we're having guests."

"It's in there," Lucy told her.

"You run on upstairs and check the rooms," Mama said to Lucy as she reached for her good apron. "Open the doors to let some heat in, and take the feather duster with you and make sure everything looks tidy and fresh. I expect they'll want the front room since it's bigger and the sun comes in so nice in there, but we'll let them take their pick."

Lucy scurried up the stairs, opening all the bedroom doors and even checking the bathroom to make sure there were no spiders or webs in the sink or the big claw-foot bathtub. Everything seemed to be in good order, but she wished it was summer so she could gather some pretty flowers to put in a vase. She thought the movie star lady would like that.

She stooped to straighten out the colorful braided rug that ran down the length of the hallway. She and Grandma had made that rug from long strips of old fabric last winter. Lucy did the braiding and Grandma did the sewing. It was supposed to keep the sounds of footsteps quieter up there, but Lucy thought it mostly looked pretty and festive.

She was just coming down the stairs when she heard someone at the front door. Lucy rushed to answer it. "Hello," she said eagerly. "I forgot to tell you, I'm Lucy."

"Pleased to meet you, Lucy. My name's Veronica." She jerked her thumb toward the man behind her. "And this is George."

"Pleased to meet you, Lucy." He leaned down to shake her hand.

Lucy was leading them into the front room just as Mama came through the dining room. She still had on her working clothes, and Lucy could tell she was uncomfortable. Probably even more so when she saw how fancy Veronica looked.

"This is George and Veronica," Lucy told Mama.

"Lucy, where are your manners? You don't call grown-ups by their first names."

"That's my fault," Veronica said. "But, really, I like to be

18

called by my first name. It makes me feel like an old schoolmarm to be called ma'am or missus." She elbowed George.

"George is fine for me." He smiled down at Lucy. "Since we're among friends."

"Mama's real name is Miriam," Lucy told them. "Isn't that a pretty name?"

"It's very nice," George said. "Nice to meet you, Miriam."

"Aren't they nice?" Lucy looked at Mama and could tell that something was bothering her. Maybe it was that this couple was nothing like their usual boarders.

"Mr. Hempley from the garage gave us a ride here," Veronica said. "He left my other suitcase on the porch for me."

"I hope we're not imposing on you." George removed his hat. "We met Lucy in town and she said you had rooms available."

"We have plenty of room." Mama made her polite face— not exactly a smile, but not unpleasant either. "I hope you'll make yourselves at home. Lunch will be ready in about half an hour . . . if you'd like to freshen up a bit. There's a guestbook in the dining room for you to register in." Now she nodded toward the stairway where Lucy was waiting. "Lucy can show you where the rooms are located, and you can take your pick." Mama stepped back. "Now if you'll excuse me, I need to help my mother prepare lunch."

As the man went out to fetch the other suitcases, Veronica patted Lucy on the head and smiled. "This is a nice little place you got here, doll."

The man returned with two more suitcases. They were tan and white and matched the smaller one that Veronica carried in one hand. Lucy wished she could see what was inside those pretty bags and wondered what Veronica might say if Lucy offered to help her unpack.

"I hope you both enjoy your stay here." Suddenly Lucy felt as if she were playing a part in a movie. Perhaps like Shirley Temple in *The Little Colonel*. "Now I will show you to your room." Holding her head high, she led them up the stairs, taking them from room to room and explaining every single detail, including how the pipes might sometimes rattle if air got trapped inside. "You just give it a good whack like this"—she hit the exposed pipe that went to the bathtub—"and it should quiet right down for you."

"I've known plumbing like that before," George told her.

"We have an outhouse too," Lucy explained. "Sometimes it comes in handy, but it can be awful cold this time of year." She stopped by the front bedroom now. "This room is really the best one." She proudly pointed to the large window. "Mama says it gets the best light in here."

"Why don't you take this room," George said to Veronica.

"Thank you." She rewarded him with a pretty smile as he set her suitcase next to the door.

"I'll take the one in the back," George told Lucy. "I like the way it looks out over the apple trees."

Lucy tried not to show her surprise, but she hadn't expected them to want *two* rooms. Most married couples shared a room together. However, she knew that Mama should be pleased by this arrangement because it meant more money, since they charged by the room as well as the meal. Lucy had imagined these people were rich. It seemed she was right. She just hoped they'd stay for a whole week or even more.

"You make yourselves comfortable," Lucy said, imitating Mama. She considered offering to help Veronica unpack but was afraid that might sound too nosy. "I should go down and set the table now."

But by the time Lucy reached the dining room, Mama was nearly finished setting the table. To Lucy's surprise, she'd put out the good china dishes—the ones with the gold and black design around the edges. "The table looks real pretty," Lucy told her. "George and Veronica should like it a lot."

"That's all?" Mama frowned as she adjusted a teacup. "Just *George* and *Veronica*?"

"Yes." Lucy nodded. "George and Veronica."

Mama looked doubtful. "Didn't they tell you their last name, Lucy?"

"I guess I forgot to ask," Lucy admitted, "but you heard them tell me to call them by their first names. Is that all right, Mama?"

"Well, I suppose so. If that's what they want. However, I don't generally care for you calling adults by their first names."

"I know." Lucy was about to tell Mama how George and Veronica were using two rooms upstairs, but Grandma stuck her head in the swinging door that led to the kitchen. "Miriam," she said, "I need your help in here, please."

"You go wash up," Mama told Lucy. "Then you can fill the water glasses for me."

Before long, the new boarders had returned downstairs and everyone was seated around the dining room table where Mama

21

bowed her head to say grace. They made small talk about the weather and traveling as the food was passed around, but the conversation grew quiet as they ate. Lucy was seated across from George and Veronica so she had a good view of their exciting new guests. Veronica had removed her fur-trimmed coat and now wore a shiny dress that was almost the same color as purple irises in the springtime. She also had on a necklace and earrings that looked like real diamonds, but Lucy couldn't be sure about that since she'd never seen real diamonds before. No matter, Veronica was still the most glamorous person Lucy had ever seen in real life. Lucy wished that Clara still lived down the road so she could see her too.

Lucy glanced over to where Mama was sitting in her usual spot at the end of the table closest to the kitchen. She liked to sit there so that she could fetch things more easily. Lucy knew it was probably wrong to compare Mama to Veronica, but she just couldn't help herself. Mama looked kind of washed out today. Sort of like when Lucy's favorite red gingham blouse got left in the sun too long and the color got drained right out of it. Even Mama's dress looked more faded and worn than usual. Plus Mama's light brown hair, pulled back in its usual bun, seemed sadly drab too. Still, Mama's eyes were pretty—and even bluer than Veronica's—although Veronica's eyelashes were much blacker, more fancy somehow. But, Lucy reminded herself, mothers weren't supposed to look like Veronica—and Mama was simply Mama. And really, she was a lot prettier than all the other mothers in Maple Grove.

"This is about the best chicken and dumplings I've ever had," George proclaimed. "My compliments to the chef."

"Grandma does most of the cooking," Lucy told him. "But Mama can cook too," she added quickly.

George told them about his car and how he felt like a fool to have let the radiator boil dry like he did. "My father used to warn me about that very thing. I really should've known better. That's what comes of driving too many hours, but I'd really hoped to make it to Los Angeles before nightfall."

"What takes you to Los Angeles?" Grandma asked.

"I hope to find work there," he told her.

"What sort of work?" she asked.

"That's a good question." George's mouth twisted to one side as they waited for him to answer. "You see, I'd been in college back east . . . back before Black Friday. I'd been in law school, but like a lot of other students, my family's funds ran out before I could finish my degree. So I took a clerical job in an insurance firm and worked there for the past six years, finishing my schooling and trying to save enough to take my bar exams and get a practice started. As luck had it, the insurance company went under last spring, and I haven't been able to find work since. I've heard that California has more job opportunities."

"Not to mention more sunshine," Veronica added. "Did you know that California is so warm and sunny that you can actually grow orange trees right in your own backyard?" She sighed dreamily. "Imagine that."

"That does sound lovely," Mama said. "I'm sure you'll be very happy there."

"If I can ever get there." George dismally shook his head. "I'm afraid my car's engine is going to take nearly until Christmas to get fixed. And the holidays aren't a good time to go job hunting."

"You can stay here for Christmas," Lucy said suddenly. "We have plenty of room."

George laughed. "I appreciate the offer, little lady. I just hope I don't have to take you up on it."

"I don't *want* to stay here until Christmas." Veronica made a pout toward George. "Surely it won't take that long to fix your silly old car, will it?"

He shrugged, but the look on his face was hard to read.

"Well, one way or another, I plan to get myself out to California," Veronica proclaimed. "There must be a train station nearby."

"Of course." Grandma reached for the butter. "Flagstaff has a perfectly good train station."

"How far are we from Flagstaff?" Veronica asked.

"It's about twenty miles," Mama told her.

"Surely I could get a train to California from there." Veronica made a long sigh. "That is, if I could get myself to Flagstaff."

Lucy stared at her. "You'd go to California by yourself?"

Veronica just laughed. "Well, of course."

"Would you care for more chicken and dumplings?" Mama asked George in a stiff-sounding voice.

"Don't mind if I do."

As Mama quietly ladled out another helping, Lucy could tell by the firm set of Mama's mouth that she was upset about something.

"I have to get to Hollywood," Veronica explained, "because

I plan to become a movie actress. You know, like Jean Harlow . . . Myrna Loy . . . Barbara Stanwyck."

"Is that so?" Grandma adjusted her glasses, peering more carefully at Veronica.

"You're pretty enough to be an actress," Lucy said shyly.

"Well, thank you very much." Veronica rewarded her with a shining smile.

"Do you know how to act?" Mama asked her. "I mean, have you participated in dramatic productions or theater before?"

Veronica waved her hand. "Oh, sure. I've done a few things. Nothing terribly impressive. But that doesn't matter so much in the motion picture business. Most of all the directors are looking for the right kind of face." She turned her head to one side and tipped her chin upward. "I've been told I'm highly photogenic and I'd look good on the big screen."

Lucy nodded eagerly. "I think you'd look just fine in a movie."

Veronica began to talk about a motion picture she'd recently seen. "Clark Gable and Claudette Colbert were in it," she explained with wide-eyed enthusiasm. "It was called *It Happened One Night*, and it was about a couple who were taking a road trip." She giggled. "Kind of like George and me." She went on to say how everyone got very confused, and then the woman was going to marry someone else, and Veronica chattered on and on until Lucy felt lost—happily lost. She thought she could listen to Veronica talking about movies forever.

"Well." Mama said this in a way that suggested she'd heard enough. "That is all very interesting, but if you'll excuse me, I have some work to attend to now." She scooted back her chair and stood. "Lucy, you will help your grandmother clear the table, please." Mama left, and the meal and the interesting conversation seemed to be over too.

"I'm plumb worn out from all the traveling I've been doing." Veronica set her napkin on the table. "I do believe I'll catch up on some beauty rest this afternoon."

George thanked Grandma for the delicious meal and excused himself as well. Grandma reminded them both to sign in at the registration book on the buffet table, and then she and Lucy began to clear the table and wash the dishes.

"I 'spect your mama won't be using the good china for the next meal," Grandma said in a funny-sounding voice.

"Why not?" Lucy asked.

Grandma just chuckled.

Lucy held up a delicate teacup and nodded. "I guess I don't mind if she uses the everyday dishes. I don't worry so much about breaking those."

"Everyday dishes are more practical."

"Do you think Veronica is pretty, Grandma?"

Her brow creased. "I suppose some people might think a woman like that is pretty . . . if you like that sort of thing."

"I think Veronica is about the prettiest person I've ever laid eyes on," Lucy confessed.

"I don't know as I'd go as far as all that."

"I think she'll probably become a real movie star too," Lucy continued with enthusiasm. "Can't you just imagine seeing Veronica's face at our movie theater in town?"

"You know I don't care much for motion pictures, Lucy. The

truth is, I'm rather surprised that George is agreeable to that kind of nonsense for his wife. He didn't strike me as that sort of fellow." Grandma made a tsk-tsk sound through her teeth. "But young people nowadays . . . I 'spect times are changing."

After the dishes were washed and dried and put back in the china cabinet, Lucy decided to take a peek at the registration book. She was curious about where George and Veronica had come from. But to her surprise, they had written down different last names. George's last name was listed as Prescott and Veronica's was Grant. Not only that, but George had written that he'd come from Chicago, Illinois, and Veronica had written St. Louis, Missouri. Lucy knew enough about geography to know that those places were a ways apart.

"Did our guests sign in?" Mama asked as she laid some freshly ironed table linens in the drawer at the bottom of the china cabinet.

"Yes . . ." Lucy gave her a quizzical look.

"Is something wrong?"

Lucy shrugged, then closed the guestbook. If something was wrong, she wasn't sure she wanted Mama to know about it. Not just yet anyway. Already Mama seemed slightly disturbed by their new guests. Lucy suspected that Mama might not be too happy about renting rooms to movie stars, or *almost* movie stars. But Lucy thought it was terribly exciting. It was also an answer to her prayers. Besides that, didn't they need the money?

Fortunately, Mama didn't question her further. Instead she asked Lucy to bring some firewood out to the barn where she was working on laundry this afternoon. Some people might think it strange to do laundry in a barn, but their barn wasn't used for animals anymore. The only livestock they had these days was old Beulah the milk cow, who mostly lived in a loafing shed near the barn, and the chickens. The barn had long since been cleaned and swept and was where Mama kept their wringer washer and ironing board as well as several clotheslines that were strung back and forth. During the winter, a woodstove was kept burning to warm the barn enough for the laundry to dry.

As Lucy piled firewood into her wagon, she daydreamed about Veronica Grant starring in a motion picture playing at the Maple Grove movie theater. It would be so exciting to stand in the ticket line and tell everyone within earshot about how the famous actress had actually slept at their house.

Lucy wished that school wasn't already let out for Christmas vacation, because she wanted the chance to tell Helen Krausner all about it. She wouldn't brag, exactly, since bragging wasn't very nice. But she would happily tell Helen all about the almost movie star who was staying at their house. She would carefully describe just how beautiful and well dressed Veronica was and how she let Lucy call her by her first name and all sorts of things. Not to be mean, but just to show Helen that she wasn't the only one with interesting things to talk about. Helen always acted like she was better than everyone else, but Lucy was certain that Helen had never had someone as glamorous as Veronica Grant stay at her house. Really, it was almost as good as having a pony!

3

Do you need some help with that?"

Lucy looked up from where she was using both hands in an attempt to tug her heavily loaded wagon out of a muddy rut in the middle of the driveway. George peered down at her with a curious expression. He'd changed out of his brown suit and was now wearing gray corduroy trousers and a dark green sweater. Without waiting for her to answer, he picked up the back end of the wagon and helped her to move it past the rut.

"Thanks." She smiled at him.

"Where are you taking that wood?" he asked as he walked alongside her.

She explained about Mama's laundry setup in the barn.

"No kidding?" He scratched his head. "Your mother is a very enterprising woman."

Lucy frowned. "Enterprising?"

He grinned. "That means she's a hard-working business-woman."

"Oh." She nodded. "My daddy used to take care of everything. But when he died, Mama had to work harder than ever."

"I'm sorry to hear about your father, Lucy." Now he reached down and took the handle of the wagon from her. "Why don't you let me help with that?"

Lucy didn't protest as he continued pulling the firewood toward the barn. "Can I ask you a question?" she said quietly.

"Sure." He paused to look at her.

"Why do you and Veronica have different names?"

He looked somewhat bewildered.

"I peeked at the guestbook," she confessed. "Veronica's last name is Grant and yours is Prescott."

He still seemed slightly confused, almost as if he was surprised by this himself. But then his eyes lit up like someone turned the lights on. "Oh, I think I understand. You must have assumed that Veronica and I were husband and wife."

Now Lucy felt confused, but she just nodded dumbly.

"Veronica and I aren't married, Lucy. We simply met on the road."

"You met on the road?" Lucy tried to imagine them meeting on the road, shaking hands, exchanging names.

"It's a long story, but Veronica needed a ride and I was going her way. That's how we met."

Lucy didn't know what to say as she slid open the barn door and waited for George to pull the loaded wagon inside before she slid it closed again.

"Oh?" Mama looked up from her ironing board in surprise.

"George is helping me," Lucy explained as she pointed over to the big old woodstove.

George rolled the wagon over and started unloading the wood onto the nearby pile.

"Well, thank you," Mama told him in a stiff voice.

"This is quite some setup you've got here." George looked around the barn with an approving expression. "What a great idea for drying laundry in the wintertime."

"Yes, well, we don't usually have our guests out here." Mama pressed her lips together as she smoothed the front of her old apron.

"I'm sorry to intrude." George stepped back as if he were feeling uncomfortable. "I was just out for a walk, and it looked like Lucy needed a hand."

"George said you're *enterprising*," Lucy told Mama, trying out her new word and hoping to put things more at ease. Why was Mama acting so contrary today?

"Enterprising is one way of putting it." Mama was using a tight-sounding voice. "I just do what needs to be done." She turned her attention back to where she was ironing a man's white shirt. "So if you will kindly excuse me."

"Sorry to bother you, ma'am." George tipped his hat, then made a quick exit.

"*Mama.*" Lucy went over by the ironing board after the door was closed. "Why are you being rude to our guests today?"

Mama used the back of her hand to push a wisp of hair off her damp forehead. "Was I being rude?"

"It seemed like it to me." Lucy peered curiously at her.

31

Mama sighed. "I suppose it's because I don't completely approve of our guests, Lucy. I don't like the idea of a man letting his wife run off to Hollywood to become a movie actress. It just doesn't sit well with me, and I think—"

"But Veronica's *not* his wife," Lucy clarified.

Mama looked at her with startled eyes. *"What?"*

"George just told me that they met on the road. They're not married at all." Lucy thought that this should fix everything in Mama's mind.

"They're *not* married?" Mama set her iron down with a thud.

"No, Mama."

"Well!" And just like that, without even moving the iron from the shirt it was still resting on, Mama stormed out of the barn without even bothering to close the door.

Feeling alarmed and somewhat responsible for whatever was about to happen, Lucy set the heavy iron upright, then trailed after her angry mother. "What's wrong, Mama?" she called, but Mama was walking fast, and in a moment they were in the kitchen where Mama was talking quickly to Grandma, using words like *morals* and *scruples* and *conscience* and *ethics* and saying how nobody seemed to have them anymore and what was the world coming to anyway.

Mama threw her hands up in the air. "They are not even married," she proclaimed as if it were a crime.

"Oh my!" Grandma looked alarmed now. "What are you going to do about it, Miriam?"

Mama was pacing back and forth in the kitchen now, wringing her hands and shaking her head. "I don't know. I just don't know."

"You could throw them out," Grandma said.

Lucy bit her lip. *"Throw them out?"* she repeated. "Why would we throw them out?"

Mama's frown lines deepened. "They are a bad influence on you, Lucy. As your mama, I can't let them stay here like this."

"Why?" Lucy asked. "Is it because Veronica wants to be a movie actress?"

Mama knelt down now, looking Lucy directly in the eyes. "No, that's not the reason. Oh, I don't really approve of that exactly, and certainly not under these circumstances. But it's not a reason to throw them out."

"Then *why*, Mama?" Lucy felt close to tears now. "I prayed for boarders, just like you said, and God sent them to us. Why would you throw them out?"

Still down at Lucy's level, Mama pressed her lips together and looked up at Grandma, as if she thought she might have the answer.

"It's complicated, Lucy," Grandma said slowly. "Your mama and I don't approve of a couple sharing a room together if they're not married, and it's just—"

"But George and Veronica aren't sharing a room together," Lucy exclaimed. "Veronica is staying in the front room and George took the one in back."

"Oh." Mama stood back up, folding her arms across her front.

"So . . . can they stay?" Lucy asked hopefully.

Mama and Grandma looked at each other, but they still looked uneasy. "I don't know for sure, Lucy."

"But we need the money, Mama. You said we do."

"Why don't you go speak to them?" Grandma suggested to Mama. "Get to the bottom of it."

Mama firmly nodded. "I'll do that."

Lucy started to go with her, but Grandma put a hand on her shoulder. "You stay here with me," she said quietly. "This is grown-up business."

Lucy stayed in the kitchen, helping Grandma to make piecrust while Mama was gone. But as Lucy was rolling out the dough, she noticed George outside. It looked like he was coming back from his walk. "I guess Mama hasn't talked to George yet," she told Grandma, pointing out the kitchen window.

"That might be easier." Grandma shook her head. "She and Veronica can talk woman to woman."

Lucy wished she could overhear the conversation. More than that she hoped Mama wasn't saying anything rude to Veronica. Even if Mama didn't approve of movie actresses, it seemed wrong to be mean to her. What if Veronica took offense and decided to leave? Besides them needing the money, Lucy didn't want Veronica to go.

"Well, that's all settled," Mama said as she rejoined them in the kitchen.

"What did you decide?" Grandma asked.

Lucy stayed quietly put, hoping she might go unnoticed as she slowly moved the rolling pin across the dough on the kitchen table. Like Grandma sometimes said, Lucy just wanted to be like a fly on the wall as the grown-ups talked.

"Lucy was right," Mama told Grandma. "George and Veronica are not married. And they are not sharing a room. Veronica claims that they met while traveling. It seems Veronica needed a ride and George offered her one. Apparently there was no romance involved." Mama made an exasperated-sounding sigh. "At least not yet, anyway. But when I voiced my concerns, Veronica assured me there would be no"—Mama cleared her throat—"no degeneracy going on. And I made it perfectly clear that I will tolerate none."

Lucy wasn't sure what degeneracy meant and had no intention of asking, but based on the tone of Mama's voice, she suspected it was not a good thing. Mostly she was relieved that Veronica Grant was being allowed to stay on with them.

"Are you going to speak to George?" Grandma asked quietly.

"I don't think that will be necessary." Mama was halfway out the back door now. "I have the woman's word."

"Well." Grandma slapped the flour off her hands. "I guess that takes care of that."

After the pies were in the oven, Lucy slipped upstairs. She knew she was supposed to go up there only to replace linens or tend to the needs of guests, but she told herself that it was possible the towels needed freshening by now. Mostly she was hoping that she'd get a chance to say something to Veronica. Just in case she was feeling bad about what Mama had said.

"Hello, doll," Veronica called out as Lucy walked quietly down the hallway. "What are you up to?"

Lucy smiled at her. "Just checking to see if you need anything. Towels or soaps or anything? Or if you'd like a cup of tea?" They didn't usually bring tea to their boarders, but Veronica seemed special.

"Tea?" Veronica's blue eyes sparkled. "Yes, that would be lovely, thank you. I take just a spoonful of sugar, please."

Excited at the prospect of delivering a cup of tea to Veronica, Lucy scampered downstairs and explained her plan to Grandma.

"Tea?" Grandma scowled. "She expects you to serve her tea in her room?"

Lucy shrugged. "It was kind of my idea."

Grandma's scowl was replaced with amusement. "Oh, it was, was it?"

Lucy grinned and nodded.

"Well, just this once. No need to tell your mama about it." She nodded to the stove. "The kettle is hot, and you know where the tea is."

"I'll use an everyday cup and saucer," Lucy promised.

"That would be wise."

Before long, Lucy was carefully going up the stairs with the steaming cup of tea in both hands, trying to keep the amber liquid from slopping over the sides. "Here you go," she said as she carried it into Veronica's room.

"You are an angel." Veronica took the cup and saucer from her with a grateful smile. "I was just feeling plumb worn out from all the traveling and everything I've been through these past few days. I'd say you're just what the doctor ordered, doll."

Lucy smiled happily. "Was it exciting traveling?"

"Oh, it was exciting at first." Veronica sat down on one of the chairs flanking the window and tipped her golden head toward the other. "Do you want to sit with me?"

Lucy nodded eagerly and sat down. She didn't want to be rude, but Veronica's silky, lilac-colored dressing gown and matching bedroom slippers were so elegant and glamorous looking, it was hard not to stare. Outside of the movies, Lucy had never seen anything like them before. She wondered what Helen Krausner would say.

"You see, I started out my trip with a friend." Veronica reached for a strand of shining hair and twisted it around her finger so that it curled just like a perfect *C* beside her dainty pink ear. "At least I *thought* he was a friend. Marshall told me that he was going to manage my acting career, and that he had connections in Hollywood, and that he was going to make me into a star." She looked upward and sighed. "But he turned out to be a dirty rotten scoundrel—a liar and a thief."

Lucy's eyes grew wide. "A liar and a thief?"

Veronica nodded as she sipped her tea. "Yes. He stole money from me. We got into a big fight over it, and I told him I no longer wanted to travel with him." Her thin eyebrows arched high. "So he pulled over—right in the middle of nowhere—and he threw me and my luggage out! Right along the side of the road! Can you believe that?"

Lucy shook her head. "What did you do?"

"I was in shock at first. I mean, what was I supposed to do? Out there in the middle of nowhere with not a car in sight. But then I remembered a scene from that movie—you know, the one I told you about earlier. I was just about to do what Claudette Colbert did, when along came this pretty yellow car. The nice driver stopped and asked if I needed help. And that is how I met up with George." She giggled. "In fact, I think George looks an awful lot like Clark Gable. Don't you think so too?"

Lucy shrugged. "I don't know who Clark Gable is."

Veronica laughed. "Well, you will, doll. Believe you me, that man will be around for quite some time. And I'd wager that someday you'll see Clark Gable and me right up there on the silver screen together."

"I can't wait!"

"Anyway, back to my story. After he rescued me out on the open highway, George and I traveled for nearly two days straight just to make it this far, and then his silly old car had to go and break down on us this morning." She frowned. "I still don't know what I'm going to do about that."

"About what?"

"About getting myself to Hollywood, of course."

"Maybe you can just stay here for a while," Lucy suggested hopefully. "You said you were tired and needed your beauty rest. Why not get some beauty rest right here?"

"For a little girl, you're a smart one, aren't you?"

Lucy smiled.

"Now that your mother understands that"—she giggled in a nervous way—"that there is no sort of impropriety going on here, well, maybe I'll do just like you said. I'll get myself all rested up and refreshed real nice. Then I'll be at my very best when I head off to Hollywood. Perhaps we'll get lucky and George's pretty car will get its motor fixed sooner than they expected."

"Hempley's Garage is a very good place to get cars fixed." Lucy declared this as if she were an expert in such things, but mostly she just wanted to be sure Veronica stayed with them for a while. It was almost like having a motion picture right in their own house, and Lucy wanted to hear more of Veronica's interesting stories.

"Well, it's not like we had a choice in garages." She chuckled. "Don't take this wrong, but Maple Grove is a real hole in the wall."

"But it is nice and quiet here," Lucy pointed out. "A good place to rest up."

"Yes. And I can't really complain about the company either." She made a dreamy looking smile. "Besides . . . you never know . . . there's that old saying about the best-laid schemes of mice and men . . ."

"What's that mean?" Lucy asked.

"Just that . . . well, sometimes things have other ways of working themselves out, if you get my drift."

"Oh." Lucy nodded as if she understood.

Veronica yawned and stood. "Thanks for the tea, doll. It was *delish*."

Lucy jumped up to take the dishes from her.

"Now I think I'll catch a few more winks of beauty rest."

With the empty cup and saucer in hand, Lucy tiptoed from the room, closing the door quietly behind her. *Delish?* Was that short for delicious? Lucy would have to remember to use that word sometime. And maybe she'd try to make her bangs curl around her fingers the way Veronica did. There was so much she could learn from someone like Veronica. As she quietly walked down the stairs, she wondered what Veronica thought about sweet gray ponies and if she'd like to take a walk down the road with Lucy in order to see one.

4

To Lucy's dismay, Veronica did not emerge from her room until dinnertime. George had helped Lucy to pass the time with a couple games of checkers. He claimed not to be any good at checkers, and after the first game, she nearly believed him. But after the second game, she wasn't so sure. She would've challenged him to a third one, but it was time to help Grandma in the kitchen.

When they sat down to dinner, Mama was acting very prim and proper, and Lucy knew this was Mama's way of showing she was not entirely pleased with her boarders. If Mama was enjoying the boarders, she usually made cheerful small talk with them, going out of her way to make everyone feel comfortable. Tonight she was about as warm as the duck pond in January.

Fortunately, Grandma was in a talkative mood and asked George and Veronica a number of questions about themselves. But it was Veronica who kept the conversation rolling along.

She didn't mind talking about herself one bit. So far, Lucy had learned that Veronica's parents had owned a music store when Veronica was a girl. "But they had to give up the store in '31," she said sadly. "Just when I was getting good at the piano too. After the store was gone, I didn't have a piano anymore. But I can play well enough to act like I'm a pianist in a movie." With her eyes partially closed, she held her hands up over her plate and wiggled her fingers as if playing on a keyboard.

"That looks very real," Lucy told her.

"What do your parents think about your aspirations of becoming a motion picture actress?" Grandma asked as she served dessert.

"Well, my daddy threw a horrible fit. But my mother kind of likes the idea. She's a real good singer, and she used to do some acting too, back in her day. She told me if I make it big, she'll come out to California and live with me." Veronica giggled. "I don't think Daddy would much like that, though."

After dessert was finished, Lucy helped Mama to clean up the dinner things while Grandma sat in the front room with George and Veronica. Lucy wished she could join them, especially when she heard sweet ripples of Veronica's laughter floating toward the kitchen. It seemed like Mama was doing all she could to keep Lucy contained in the kitchen. Finally, after the last dish was dried and put away, Lucy was about to slip out to the front room, but Mama insisted they needed more firewood first.

Lucy considered protesting since the firewood box was nearly half full, but she realized it would probably save time (and trouble) to just hurry and fetch it. She pulled on her coat, then turned on the back porch light, hurried across the yard toward the woodpile with her wagon in tow, and started to load it up.

"Need a hand?" George asked as he joined her.

She looked up in surprise. "I, uh, I don't think Mama likes our guests to help with chores."

But he was already putting pieces onto the wagon. "I like making myself useful." For every piece she put in, George stacked several. Then he grasped the handle of the wagon. "Let me take that."

"Were you smoking out here?" she asked as they walked back.

"Just my pipe," he confessed. "Is that not allowed?"

"No, it's allowed," she said quickly. "I was just curious. My daddy used to smoke a pipe too."

"I don't smoke it a lot," he told her as they reached the back porch. "But sometimes it's a comfort." Already he was unloading the wood, stacking it onto his cradled arm. She wanted to tell him that he didn't need to do this, but it seemed too late. Instead, she opened the back door and, carrying the few pieces that were left, followed him into the bright, warm kitchen.

"What?" Mama looked at Lucy with wide eyes.

"I insisted on helping your daughter," George told her as he unloaded the wood into the firebox. "I hope you don't mind."

"Well, I . . . it's just that you're our guest." Mama hung her apron on the peg by the stove and stepped back. "We don't expect you to help."

He nodded, standing up straight. "I know you don't, ma'am. It's just that it looks like I'll be here a few days, and I find it hard to just sit around and do nothing. If I can do something

43

to keep myself busy, well, it just passes the time a little easier. That is, unless you have objections."

Mama shrugged as she folded her arms across her front with a slightly aggravated expression. "No objections, Mr. Prescott. If it helps you to pass the time, feel free."

"Like I told you earlier, please, just call me George."

Mama simply nodded, but those two creases had reappeared in her forehead again. Lucy knew what that meant.

"Maybe you'd like to play some more checkers?" Lucy suggested to George as she pushed open the door that led to the dining room. Mostly she hoped to get George out of harm's way since it looked like Mama was about to give him a piece of her mind.

"That sounds like a good plan," he told her.

Before long, Lucy and George were happily playing checkers. Veronica moved to a chair next to George, looking on and making comments in a way that made Lucy think she was trying to get George's attention. After a bit, Grandma excused herself to bed. But Mama never stepped a toe into the front room, not until it was time to announce that Lucy needed to get ready for bed too.

"We have church tomorrow," Mama announced. "As always, the guests here are invited to attend with us. Our neighbors, the Brewsters, are always happy to give us a ride."

"Church?" Veronica's brows arched high. "Well, I haven't been to church in ages."

"We have to leave by ten to make it on time," Mama told her. "Breakfast is at eight on Sundays."

"Eight?" Veronica sounded surprised.

"It's at seven on the other days," Mama told her.

Veronica laughed. "Well, don't worry about me. I rarely eat breakfast on any days."

"I wouldn't mind going to church," George said quietly. "If it's not a problem."

"It's not a problem at all," Mama said in a terse tone, "as long as you're ready to go when the Brewsters get here."

Veronica looked as if she was having second thoughts. "Perhaps I'll come too," she said. "You say we need to be ready by ten?"

"That's right," Mama told her as she took Lucy by the hand. "Good night, everyone."

It wasn't until Mama and Lucy were in Lucy's room with the door shut that Lucy decided to take a chance and speak her mind. "Mama," she began carefully as she unbuttoned her dress, "it seems that you're not being very *hospitable* to our guests." Although she didn't use the word a lot, Lucy knew what hospitable meant.

Mama blinked as she handed Lucy her nightgown.

"You and Grandma always tell me that I'm to treat our boarders with respect," she continued, "because they are our guests and we want them to feel special here."

Mama pressed her lips together but said nothing as she helped Lucy pull the flannel nightgown over her head. Lucy shivered as the cool fabric brushed against her back. She knew that eight years old was more than old enough to get ready for bed by herself, but this was always the one part of the day when she and Mama spent time together, so she never complained about Mama's help. As usual, she sat down on the hard-backed chair, waiting as Mama reached for the hairbrush and began to undo Lucy's braids, slowly brushing the hair out and then re-braiding it into one braid down Lucy's back.

"I suppose you're right, Lucy. I have been acting inhospitable."

"Why, Mama?"

"Well, as I already told you, I'm not that comfortable with our boarders."

"I think they're nice."

Mama didn't say anything as she set the brush down.

"And isn't it nice they want to go to church with us in the morning?"

"I suppose so." Her voice sounded tired.

Lucy turned around and hugged Mama tightly. "I'm ready to say my prayers," she whispered.

Mama nodded, waiting as Lucy knelt down on the rag rug next to her bed. Tonight Lucy didn't ask God to give her a pony. Instead, she thanked him for bringing their boarders to them, and then she asked God to bless everyone in their house. It wasn't until Mama had kissed her good-night and turned off the light that Lucy silently continued her prayer—and now she did ask God for a pony . . . and to bring back Mama's smile.

It was just a little before ten o'clock and as the Brewsters' big old Ford pulled up that Veronica made her appearance downstairs. Lucy was relieved that she was dressed—beautifully dressed in a scarlet red dress—and ready to go to church. George helped her into her fur-trimmed coat, and they all went outside to pile into the car. Usually Mama, Grandma, and Lucy sat in the backseat, but today Grandma sat in front with the Brewsters and Lucy offered to sit in the rumble seat. It was chilly back there, but it was well worth it for the joy of having Veronica Grant (soon-to-be movie star) in their company. Hopefully Helen Krausner would be in church today to see this.

Lucy looked over to Mr. Greenburg's field as the car rumbled past, making sure that Smoky and the "For Sale or Trade" sign were still there. To her relief, they both were. Hopefully she'd get a chance to pay him a visit tomorrow. Maybe she could talk Veronica into walking down there with her to see him too. The Greenburg farm was only two farms down, really just a nice walk if the weather was favorable.

As it turned out, the Krausners weren't at church, but Veronica Grant got plenty of curious looks from the congregation anyway. Lucy proudly took Veronica by the hand, leading her to the pew where they always sat, and then she squeezed down close to the end to be sure there was plenty of room for everyone in their row.

Lucy always enjoyed the singing part of church the best, and she was happy to share her hymnal with Veronica. She wasn't even too surprised to hear that Veronica had a pleasant soprano voice. No doubt that would be useful in the movie-making business too. Lucy tried to pay attention to the sermon, but instead she was distracted by staring at the beadwork on Veronica's gloves and found herself daydreaming about glamorous things like fancy dresses and sparkling jewelry. When it came time for the final prayer, Lucy was thankful that Pastor McHenry wasn't able to read her mind. She told God that she was sorry and she would try to pay better attention next Sunday.

After the final hymn, Pastor McHenry reminded the congregation of the upcoming events pertaining to Christmas, a little less than two weeks away. "For the children in the Christmas pageant, there will be rehearsals on Thursday and Saturday afternoons at two o'clock. Mrs. Babcock wants to remind everyone not to be late."

As they walked out to the car after greeting and visiting with friends, Veronica inquired as to whether anyone cared to stay in town to attend a matinee.

"On Sunday?" Mrs. Brewster sounded alarmed.

"No, dear," Grandma told her. "None of us will be seeing a motion picture today. Of course, you and George might have other ideas."

"Not me," George said as he opened a car door for the ladies.

"I'd be happy to go," Lucy said, knowing full well that this could get her into hot water with Mama. But the idea of seeing a movie with Veronica was too tempting.

"Not on a Sunday," Mama said sternly.

Veronica leaned over and patted Lucy's cheek. "Then we'll simply have to go another day. Maybe next Saturday."

Lucy smiled up at her. "I'd love that."

The perfectly delightful idea of going with Veronica to the movie theater, where Helen Krausner might see them together, was almost enough to keep Lucy warm all the way home. Although her nose did feel like an ice cube by the time the car rumbled up to their house.

"Let's get you inside," Mama said as she took Lucy by the hand, leading her directly to the kitchen where the fire was still burning in the stove.

"It almost feels like it could snow out there," Grandma said as she closed the door and began peeling off her heavy winter coat.

"*Snow?*" Lucy began to dance around the kitchen. "Snow for Christmas—do you really think so, Grandma? Oh, I can't wait!"

"Don't count your snowflakes before they fall," Mama warned her.

"Which reminds me . . ." Grandma looked at Lucy. "Did you tend to the chickens this morning?"

Lucy nodded. "I did. But there were no eggs today."

Mama blinked as she hung her coat by the door. "No eggs?"

"It's nearly winter solstice." Grandma moved the cast iron pot to the hottest part of the stove. "The shortest day of the year."

"That's right!" Lucy remembered from last winter—shortly after they'd purchased the laying hens from a neighboring farm. "The chickens need more sunlight to want to lay eggs. That's why there were no eggs this morning."

"You probably won't find eggs again for a while." Grandma shook her head. "Fortunately we still have a couple dozen in the cooler. I'll have to tell Mrs. Brewster that we can't sell any to her after all. I should've remembered that this always happens at Christmastime."

"Just one more reason I'll be glad when Christmas is over and done with this year." Mama reached for her apron.

"*Mama.*" Lucy let the disappointment show in her voice. "How can you say that?"

Mama looked somewhat contrite. "I'm sorry, Lucy. I know you love Christmas. It's just that . . . well, when you're a grown-up . . . things change."

"Then I *never* want to grow up," Lucy declared.

Grandma patted her head. "Then how about if you go set the table?"

As Lucy set the table, she decided that even if she had to grow up, she would never be like Mama. Not about Christmas, anyway. No, Lucy told herself as she set the plates down, she would rather be like Veronica Grant. Surely Veronica still liked Christmas. And Veronica liked going to movies—even on Sundays—and Veronica liked wearing pretty clothes and laughing and all sorts of exciting things. Veronica probably even liked sweet gray ponies!

5

After Sunday dinner, Lucy announced that she wanted to take a walk later, after she finished helping to clean up the dishes. Her intention was to stroll down to the Greenburg farm and check on Smoky. Maybe she'd even chat with Mr. Greenburg if he was around. "Would anyone like to join me?" She looked longingly at Veronica.

"Not me." Veronica stifled a yawn. "All that good food and getting up early has made me very sleepy. I think I'm going to take a little nap."

"I'd love to go stretch my legs," George said. "That is, unless I can do something to help out around here." He looked at Mama and then Grandma. "Need any firewood chopped?"

"No. No, thank you," Mama said quickly. "You go ahead and take a walk with Lucy if you like."

"Just make sure you bundle up," Grandma told them. "It's getting mighty cold out there."

"Grandma said it might snow," Lucy told George as she started to help clear the table.

George peered out the front window, then shook his head with a frown. "Well, I sure hope it holds off some. At least until my car gets fixed."

Lucy carried the dishes to the kitchen, but then Grandma shooed her out. "Go ahead and take your walk, Lucy. I'll get the dishes washed, and you can dry them when you get back."

Lucy found George and they layered on coats, scarves, and hats, then headed on down the road toward town. As they were walking, Lucy confessed her real reason for wanting to take a walk. "He's the most beautiful pony in the whole wide world," she told George. "Smoky's got the prettiest coat you've ever seen—dapple gray. And it's already soft and fuzzy. Nice and warm for winter. His eyes are big and brown. And he's very smart too. He'll come over to the fence when I call him. You'll see."

"He sounds like a great little pony. I'm surprised the owners want to sell him."

"I'm surprised too," Lucy admitted. "But I know times are hard. We had to sell almost all of our livestock."

"You had livestock?"

She nodded as she stuck a mittened hand into a coat pocket, checking to see that the big end of a carrot was still safely there. "Before my daddy died, we had cows and horses and pigs. Now we just have the chickens and one milk cow."

"Was it too hard to take care of all those animals?"

"I guess so. Mama said that someday we might get them back, though. That is, if we get the rest of our farm back."

"The *rest* of your farm?"

Lucy explained about how some of their land was being farmed by the Farleys now. "The Farleys have six boys to help out with farm chores," she told him. "For a while Mr. Farley paid us every year at harvest time for using our land. But he can't do that anymore. Mama says we're just lucky he's working it at all. Otherwise it would just go back to weeds." She pointed at the Saunderses' neglected farm. "Like that farm." She told George about Clara and her family moving away and how much she missed them. "Clara was my very best friend."

"Are there any other girls living nearby?" he asked.

"No." She sadly shook her head, explaining that the Brewsters never had children and that the Greenburg children were all grown up.

"Maybe that's why Mr. Greenburg wants to sell his pony," George suggested.

She nodded. "Maybe so." She pointed at the sign still on the fence post. "That's for Smoky," she said happily. "That must mean no one bought him yet." She ran up to the fence, climbed onto the bottom rail, and called out. Just like that, Smoky left where he'd been standing in the trees, trotting over to see her.

"Don't tell anyone," she said as she extracted a slightly fuzzy-looking carrot stub from her pocket. "But I sneaked this from the kitchen."

George chuckled. "Your secret's safe with me."

"Hello, Smoky," she said happily. "How are you doing today?"

He shook his mane as if to greet her, and she peeled off her mitten and held out the carrot stub in the palm of her hand. "It's

53

not much," she told him. "But I hope you like it." She giggled as the warm, fuzzy muzzle tickled the palm of her hand and just like magic the carrot disappeared. She patted the broad side of his cheek. "Isn't he just the most beautiful pony you've ever seen?"

George reached out and stroked Smoky's mane. "He's a very nice-looking pony, for sure. And he seems healthy too."

Lucy looked all around the field behind Smoky, hoping to spot Mr. Greenburg. But all was quiet and still today. Maybe the Greenburgs were in town. She looked up at the sky now, noticing that it was almost exactly the same color as Smoky, and then to her delighted surprise she spotted a snowflake fluttering down right in front of her. "Look at that!" she cried, pointing upward. "It's starting to snow!"

George looked up and chuckled. "You're right about that."

"Maybe we will have a white Christmas," she told him.

"Maybe so." He slowly nodded.

She remembered his concerns about getting to California in the snow. "Or maybe it's just fooling us," she said quickly. "Sometimes our weather is tricky like that. It looks like snow is coming, but then it waits a few days."

"Well, just in case, I suppose we should turn back and get home. I wouldn't want to get caught out here in a blizzard."

She climbed down from the fence. "Good-bye, Smoky," she said sadly. "I'll come back and see you again as soon as I can. Please don't let anyone buy you."

Smoky tipped his head up and down as if agreeing to this. Lucy reluctantly turned away, and she and George headed back toward home. They walked quietly for a ways before Lucy spoke up. "Please don't tell Mama that I took you to see Smoky," she said suddenly.

"Why not?"

Lucy considered this. "Well, Mama doesn't want me to keep wishing for a pony. She thinks it's impossible. And Grandma says ponies are only for rich people. But I've been praying for a pony, and Pastor McHenry says God can do impossible things." She peered up at George. "Do you think God will answer my prayer?"

George's mouth was in a firm line now. "Yes . . ." he said slowly. "I definitely think God will answer your prayer, Lucy. But sometimes God's answer isn't the answer we want. Sometimes God's answer is no . . . or wait."

Lucy kicked a stone on the road and sighed. "I know. Grandma says that exact same thing sometimes. But maybe God will say yes."

"Maybe so." George pointed up at the sky. "It looks like this snow is really coming now. Maybe we should walk faster."

By the time they got home, everything, including Lucy and George, was spotted in white snowflakes. Pausing on the front porch to brush the snow off, Lucy suddenly remembered Smoky. "Do you think he'll be okay?" she said quietly to George.

"Who?"

"Smoky." She imagined the pony coated with snow, shivering in the wind.

George got a thoughtful look, then nodded. "Yes. Smoky has a thick wooly coat. I'm sure he'll be just fine."

Lucy hoped that George was right. She'd never worried about

farm animals being out in the cold like that before, but she knew that she wouldn't want to have to live outside when it was snowing and blowing like it was starting to do now. And even though Mama used most of the barn for her laundry business, there were still some nice warm stalls in the back. Surely it would be all right for a pony to use one of them . . . just to come in from the cold. Lucy would keep it nice and clean.

Lucy was pleased to wake up to a white, wintry world on Monday morning. It was only a few inches so far, but it was beautiful. Like a gigantic frosted cake.

"Sit still," Mama said as Lucy kicked the heels of her boots against the kitchen stool. "Let me get this last braid finished."

"I just can't wait to go outside," Lucy said happily. "I'm going to make a snow angel first thing. Then a snowman if the snow is sticky enough."

"Just make sure you see to the chickens first. And bring in some more wood."

"Yes, Mama." Lucy pulled on her coat, searching her pockets for mittens. Before long she was bundled up and on her way outside with a bucket of chicken food. The air was crisp and cold, and the sound of snow crunching beneath her boots filled her with high hopes. She always felt excited over the first snow, and to have it before Christmas was a real treat.

"Good morning, Lucy."

She jumped to see George coming around the corner of the barn. "What are you doing out here?" she asked.

"Just taking a walk." He jerked his thumb behind him. "I broke the ice in the chickens' water trough. I hope that's all right."

"Sure." She grinned. "Thanks. I'm just on my way to feed them now."

He turned around and walked back with her. "I noticed an old Model T back behind the barn."

"That was my daddy's car." Lucy opened the gate to the chicken yard and went inside. George hadn't just broken the ice; he'd refilled the water and even cleaned the snow out of the food trough so it was all ready for her to dump the kitchen scraps. The hungry hens gathered around her feet as she spread the food out for them. "You girls need to start laying eggs again," she told them.

"Why aren't they laying eggs?" George held the gate open for her, then securely latched it closed after she came out.

Lucy explained about the winter solstice, and he rubbed his chin with a thoughtful expression. "So they need sunlight to lay eggs?"

"That's what Grandma says. It always happens right around Christmastime."

"What if we rigged up a light bulb inside their coop?"

"A light bulb?" She giggled as she tried to imagine a light bulb in the henhouse.

"You could turn it on just before the sun sets. Leave it on for an hour or so. Maybe the chickens would think it was still daytime and reward you with some eggs."

"Do you really think that would work?"

"It might be worth a try." He pointed to the barn. "I noticed there's electricity running from the house to the barn."

"Mama had the electric put in so she could do her laundry out there."

"Well, it wouldn't be hard to run a cord from the barn to the chicken coop and get a light set up. I could give it a try if you think it's a good idea."

She nodded eagerly. "It's a swell idea."

"Would your mother mind if I poked around to find what I need for the light?"

"I think Mama would be real happy if we started getting eggs again."

"About that car," he said as they walked back to the house. "Does it run at all?"

"No, it's been broken down for a long, long time. Mr. Brewster offered to buy it once, but Mama said no. Now she'd gladly sell it, but he can't afford to buy it anymore. And no one else wants a car that doesn't run." She stopped walking and set the chicken bucket down. "I'm glad because sometimes I like to sit in it and I pretend like I'm driving." She flopped down on her back, and George's eyes nearly popped out.

"What's wrong?" He bent over and stared. "Are you okay?"

"I'm making a snow angel," she explained as she flapped her arms and legs.

With a quizzical expression, he pulled out his pipe and watched her.

"See?" She stood, proudly pointing to the angelic image in the snow.

"Very nice." He lit his pipe and smiled.

She went over to where the snow angel head was and drew in a halo. "There. Perfect."

"Do you think your mother would mind if I took a look at the old car?" He let out a puff of sweet-smelling smoke. "My dad used to have a car almost exactly like it, and if I'm lucky, I might be able to get it running again."

"*Really?*" She brushed the snow off her coat sleeves.

"It's a possibility."

"I sure wish it could run again." She sighed. "I remember how I used to ride to town in it with my daddy . . . back when I was a little girl."

His pipe slowly moved up and down like he was thinking hard.

"Maybe we shouldn't tell Mama about it, though." She glanced over to the house. "Just so we don't get her hopes up. You know, in case you can't fix it."

He removed his pipe, placing a forefinger over his lips. "I won't tell if you won't tell."

She nodded. "It's a deal."

As they were finishing lunch, George announced that he planned to walk to town to check on the progress of his car's repairs. "Let me know if there's anything I can bring home for anyone."

"No, thank you," Mama primly told him. "Lucy did the shopping for us on Saturday."

"But you might let George drop off your laundry parcels," Grandma suggested to Mama. "That would save you a—"

"Oh, that's all right," Mama said. "I don't mind the walk."

"I'd be pleased to deliver your parcels for you," George told her.

"But I wouldn't want to bother you with—"

"It's no bother," he assured her. "Just write down the addresses for me, and I'll gladly drop them off. I plan to leave around two."

Mama started to protest again, but this time Veronica interrupted. "Why don't you just use the telephone, George?" she suggested. "Simply call the garage and check on your automobile. Save yourself a senseless walk."

He shook his head. "I'd prefer to walk. I need the exercise."

"Do you want any company?" Lucy offered hopefully.

"I need you to stay home and help Grandma and me," Mama told her.

Lucy frowned but didn't say anything.

"Maybe next time," George said gently.

"Yes, maybe next time." Mama's voice was firm.

"You didn't invite little old me to go to town with you, George," Veronica said in a sugary voice.

George looked taken aback by this. "Well, I—I suppose I assumed you wouldn't want to walk out in the snow."

"You know me too well." She made a pouting face. "You're right about walking in the snow. I don't have the right sort of shoes."

"Mama could loan you her work boots," Lucy suggested.

Mama looked as if she was about to choke, but Veronica just laughed. "Really, now, Lucy, can you imagine me in your mama's work boots?"

"Of course not." Mama began clearing the table. "What a ridiculous idea."

"Well, I'm sure they're just fine for you," Veronica said apologetically. "You need sturdy boots to work on a farm."

Mama excused herself. As she went through the swinging door, Lucy felt pretty sure she wouldn't come back out again.

"I do wish there was some other way to get to town," Veronica said to George. "Do you suppose there's a taxi that could come and fetch us?"

Grandma chuckled. "Not in Maple Grove." She picked up the bread basket and butter dish and excused herself to the kitchen too.

"If I had a pony," Lucy told Veronica, "I'd let you ride it to town."

"Me on a pony?" Veronica giggled. "Now *that* would be a sight to see. I've never been on a horse in my entire life."

"What if you needed to ride a horse to be in a movie?" Lucy asked.

"Well, then I wouldn't be in that particular movie." Veronica nudged George with her elbow. "I'll bet you don't know how to ride a horse either, do you?"

"Now there's a bet you would surely lose," he told her.

"Well." She looked impressed. "You are just full of surprises, aren't you, Georgie Porgie?"

Lucy pressed her lips together as she remembered his ideas for fixing the old car. That would probably surprise Veronica too. Instead of saying anything about this, Lucy began to help clear her side of the table.

"She just gets to me," Mama was quietly saying to Grandma as Lucy came in. But seeing Lucy, Mama stopped talking.

"Did I say something wrong, Mama?" Lucy set the dishes by the sink and peered up into Mama's face.

"Oh, it was silly of you to think Veronica would wear my old boots . . . that's all."

"And to think she'd walk to town," Grandma added with a half smile. "Well, that's not very realistic."

Lucy shrugged. "She might walk to town . . . if it wasn't so cold and snowy out." The dining room was empty when she went back to get the last of the dishes. She was just about to return to the kitchen when she overheard Veronica talking to George in the front room.

"Oh, come on, George," Veronica was saying sweetly. "Just use the telephone to call and find out about your silly old car. That way you can stay here and keep me company. We can play games or listen to the radio or just visit."

"I'm sorry. I already planned to go to town."

"But it's so quiet and lonely when you're not in the house," she protested.

"Like I said, you're welcome to join me."

"You know I don't want to do that. Oh, Georgie Porgie, you're just a big meanie," she teased, "but I'll come up with a way to get back at you. You know I will."

"I'm sure you will."

"Will you bring me back something?" she pleaded in childlike voice. "A candy or some kind of special treat?"

"Sure. Tell me what you want and I'll bring it back."

Feeling guilty for eavesdropping and just a little bit jealous that George was going to bring Veronica a treat, Lucy made her way back into the kitchen. Mama had gone out to get the laundry parcels, and Grandma had already started on the dishes.

"Do you think Veronica and George are falling in love?" she asked Grandma as she set the cups and saucers on the counter.

"Falling in love?" Grandma peered curiously at Lucy. "What put that kind of an idea in your head?"

"Helen Krausner is always talking about falling in love," Lucy confessed. "But I don't think I've ever seen it happen. Not for real."

"I suppose they could be falling in love." Grandma squeezed soapy water out of the dishrag. "Although I think George is too sensible for that flibbertigibbet."

"Flibbertigibbet?" Lucy was surprised.

Grandma chuckled. "I suppose that's not very nice to say about our guest, Lucy. I hope I don't hear you repeating it."

"I'd never say that about Veronica," Lucy assured her. "I like Veronica." But even as she said this, Lucy wasn't so sure. She didn't think she liked Veronica quite as much as when she'd first met her. She wasn't even sure why.

6

After helping in the kitchen, Lucy went to her room to work on this year's Christmas presents. She'd started crocheting the potholders for Grandma in October. Made from various colors of yarn that she'd found in a box in the attic, their colorful stripes reminded her of rainbows. At first she thought she only had enough yarn for two potholders, but to her surprise there was enough for a third.

For Mama, she'd made a picture frame out of sticks and pinecones that she'd gathered out in the woods. Inside the frame was a pencil drawing that Lucy had made of a cactus wren. The small, spotted wren was the Arizona state bird, and Lucy had meticulously drawn it from a picture she'd found in a bird book at school. She'd also embroidered a white linen handkerchief with birds for Mama. One was a beautiful red cardinal and the other a bluebird. Mama loved birds of all kinds, and Lucy couldn't wait to see her face when she opened these presents on Christmas morning.

But with George and Veronica staying with them, hopefully until Christmas, Lucy had decided to make some more Christmas presents as well. For Veronica, she was making a pincushion. Oh, she knew that Veronica probably didn't know how to sew, but she had some beautiful brooches that she liked to wear, and Lucy thought perhaps she would use the pincushion for those.

For George she had started to make a pipe holder. Of course, she had no idea if he would have any use for such a thing or even if there was such a thing as a pipe holder, but it seemed like a good idea. She'd started with an old wooden cigar box she'd found in the attic. First she took it apart, and she was now trying to transform some of the pieces into a rack of sorts. Plus she'd found a picture of a handsome black racehorse in an old magazine and carefully cut it out and glued it to the back of the holder. Now she was gluing some sticks around the horse like a little frame, and really, it was becoming a rather handsome piece.

It was just getting dusky when Lucy remembered she hadn't fed the chickens this afternoon. Pulling on her boots and coat, she grabbed the bucket by the back door and hurried outside. As far as she knew, George hadn't returned from town yet. But when she reached the chicken coop, she was surprised to see that light was coming from the coop area. Filling the food trough, she heard the sound of crunching snow coming from around the backside of the barn. Worried it might be a wild animal, she lifted up the bucket, ready to throw it if needed. But to her relief it was only George.

"You scared me," she said as she lowered the bucket.

"I'm sorry. But I thought I heard someone over here. What do you think of our light?"

"I think it's great. I hope it works."

"I figure we should only leave it on for an hour. So they can get used to it."

"Do you think it'll work?"

He tipped his head sideways. "I have no idea, but I guess we'll find out. We just need to remember to come out here to turn it off after dinner. How about if I take care of that while I'm here? I'll just say I'm going out to smoke my pipe."

"Sounds good to me." She looked toward where he'd come around from behind the barn. "What are you doing back there?"

He held up a wrench with a sheepish grin. "Working on your dad's car."

"Really?"

He nodded. "Picked up a couple things at Hempley's Garage and couldn't wait to see if they worked."

"Do they?"

"We'll see."

"You sound like Mama."

He chuckled. "I'll take that as a compliment."

"Speaking of Mama, I'd better get back inside and set the table."

"Not yet." He came over and opened the gate to the chicken yard, waiting for her to come out before he closed it. "I have something for you first." He reached in his pocket now and pulled out something wrapped in brown paper.

"What?" she said eagerly.

"Just some peppermints." He held up his forefinger. "But not until after dinner."

"Thank you!" She stuck it in her coat pocket, then hurried back into the house to help with dinner. But Mama was already helping Grandma, and once the table was set, they didn't need Lucy anymore.

"Why don't you go visit with Veronica?" Mama suggested. "She's sitting by herself in the front room."

"All that woman does is sleep and listen to the radio all day," Grandma said quietly as Lucy was leaving.

"Hello, Veronica," Lucy said pleasantly. She sniffed the air, noticing a strange smell. Kind of like the chicken scraps starting to go bad on a hot summer's day.

"There you are, doll." Veronica gave a pretty smile as she set a small bottle of red fingernail paint on the coffee table. Lucy hoped there were no drips on the bottle since Mama loved that table. "I was just wishing for something to amuse myself with."

"Want to play checkers?" Lucy offered.

Veronica wrinkled her nose. "I don't like board games. Besides, I just did my nails."

"Oh." Lucy sat down on the chair across from her.

"What I wouldn't give for a ride to town to see a movie tonight."

"That would be fun." Lucy nodded.

"I am hopelessly bored." Veronica blew across the tops of her blood red fingernails. "I cannot comprehend how on earth you country people manage to live like this. So isolated . . . and now all this horrid snow. I feel as if I'm trapped." She sighed.

"How I miss the city lights, the nightclubs, the glamour, the music." She made a groaning sound. "I feel like I shall start climbing the walls."

"Oh . . ." Lucy smiled to herself as she imagined Veronica in her elegant, pale blue dress climbing up the front room walls.

Veronica looked hopefully at Lucy now. "Listen, doll," she began quietly. "Maybe you can help me."

"Help you?"

Veronica leaned forward. "You're on pretty good terms with old Georgie Porgie, aren't you?"

Lucy wasn't sure how to answer, so she shrugged. "I guess so."

"Maybe you can do some sweet-talking for me."

"Sweet-talking?"

"It sounds like Georgie's car might be fixed by Wednesday."

Lucy felt a wave of disappointment. "Wednesday?"

Veronica nodded eagerly. "I plan to be dressed in my traveling clothes with everything neatly packed so that I'm ready to hit the road as soon as that sweet yellow roadster rolls up to the house. And I'd like Georgie to be on the same page."

"On the same page?"

Veronica laughed. "I want Georgie all packed and ready to go too. My thinking is that we could make Los Angeles by midnight." She sighed happily. "Imagine that. Hollywood . . . sunshine . . . orange trees. It will be like heaven."

"Oh . . ." Lucy looked down, picking at the beginnings of a hole in her work trousers. She must have caught it on the chicken wire.

"Here's what I want you to do for me." Veronica began to

map out a plan for Lucy to hint to George that he and Veronica should be on their way . . . the sooner the better for everyone. "Maybe you can let him know that Christmas is a time for families to be together and that your family won't be wanting any strangers around during the holidays."

"But you and George aren't strangers," Lucy protested.

Veronica laughed. "Well, that's real sweet, doll, but a few days from now George and I will be living a completely different life in a completely different place, and you'll still be here. In a way we'll be like strangers."

Lucy felt a lump in her throat.

"So will you do that for me?"

Lucy nodded sadly. "I guess so."

"Don't worry, doll, we won't really be strangers. I'll always remember you and how your family took me in."

"Really?" Lucy blinked at her.

"Sure. And when I'm famous, you'll go see me at the movie theater, won't you? You can tell all your friends that you're a friend of Veronica Grant." She tipped her head back and smiled as if someone were taking her photograph.

"I guess that means we won't get to go to the picture show on Saturday."

Veronica gave Lucy a sympathetic look. "I'm sorry, doll. But you understand . . . if I'm going to become a star, I must get to Hollywood."

Lucy told Veronica that she understood and that she would do what she could to help, but she didn't tell her that her heart would not be in it.

70

The next morning, Lucy was surprised to see nearly a foot of snow on the ground. At this rate, they really would have a white Christmas this year. Of course, she realized this could present its own set of problems. For one thing, Veronica wouldn't like it one bit. It might put the brakes on their trip to California. Although when Lucy had raised the subject last night, hinting about Veronica's plans, as George smoked his pipe on the porch, he had seemed unconcerned about whether they left for California on Wednesday or next week. Lucy had been relieved, but she knew Veronica would not be pleased.

Besides the snow being a problem to George and Veronica, Lucy knew it meant there would be more work to do—snow shoveling on top of all the other chores which grew more difficult in wintertime. Still, she was happy about the snow and the idea of having a white Christmas, and she hurried to get dressed and because she was anxious to check on the chickens. Maybe George's light idea had worked and the hens had laid some eggs last night. She zipped out through the kitchen and nearly collided with Mama on the back porch.

"Oh!" Mama balanced the pail of milk in her hand, managing not to spill a drop. "Careful there, Lucy."

"Sorry. I was on my way to the chickens."

"In an awful hurry too." Mama peered curiously at her. "By the way, I noticed that someone ran electricity out to the chicken coop."

Lucy bit her lip and looked down at her boots.

71

"Do you know anything about that, Lucy? Or did the chickens decide that it was about time they lived like the rest of us?"

Lucy looked up and grinned.

"Tell me, what's going on?"

Lucy quickly explained George's idea. "We were going to surprise you with it . . . I mean, if it turned out that it worked."

With a bewildered look, Mama just shook her head.

"Is it all right? I mean, that we did it without telling you?"

"Yes. It's fine. It actually sounds like a good idea." Mama reached for the door. "I'll be curious to see if it works or not."

"I'm on my way to check right now." Lucy picked up the chicken bucket, then hurried on her way. It wasn't until she was halfway to the barn that she realized someone had plowed a path through what otherwise would have been knee-deep snow. Mama must have gotten up really early this morning. To Lucy's delight, the path went all the way to the chicken coop. Not only that, but the chicken yard had been shoveled as well.

Feeling optimistic, Lucy checked the hen nests, but to her dismay there were no eggs yet. "Come on, girls," she told the sleepy hens. "If you like having your own light at night, you need to thank us with some eggs." Lucy filled their trough, but like yesterday their water had already been tended to. Surely that was not Mama's doing. Lucy rubbed a wooly mitten across her dripping nose and wondered what it would be like if George lived with them all the time. Winters could be hard in this part of the country. Last year had been bitter cold, and it hadn't taken long for Lucy's enthusiasm over the first snow to grow thin. She latched the gate closed and sighed. Well, with Christmas only a week away, she was not going to worry about that now. Maybe she would secretly pray that this weather would keep George and Veronica here until New Year's!

As usual, Veronica slept in during breakfast. The first day this happened, Lucy had felt disappointed. She never wanted to miss an opportunity to be around the glamorous Veronica Grant. But this morning she realized that meals felt more pleasant when Veronica wasn't there. It seemed that everyone at the table was more cheerful and the visiting sounded cozy and natural . . . and nice.

"Thank you for shoveling snow this morning," Mama told George as she passed him the bowl of applesauce.

"So that *was* you!" Lucy said. "I thought so."

"Unless it was your snow angel . . ." His eyes twinkled with mystery as he spooned some applesauce onto his hotcakes. "I think I saw her dancing about in the twilight this morning."

Lucy laughed. "Today I plan to make a snowman," she told everyone. "I'll sit him in front of the house, right next to the porch. I want him to be really tall too." She pointed at George. "Even taller than you."

"Need any help?"

"Sure." She took a big bite of her hotcake, eager to finish her breakfast and get outside.

"Chew your food," Grandma told her. "The snow isn't going anywhere."

True to his word, George helped her make what turned out to be the best snowman ever. Not only was he taller than George, but Mama brought out one of Daddy's old work hats and a knitted scarf to dress him with.

"Now wait," George told Lucy. "I'll run and get my camera and take a photograph of you and Mr. Snowman together."

"I want you in the picture too," Lucy exclaimed.

"But I need to take the photo—"

"Let Mama take it," Lucy said.

After George returned with his camera and explained to Mama how to use it, Lucy and George posed on either side of the giant snowman as Mama took the photograph. "When I get the film developed, I'll send you this picture," George promised.

Lucy felt sad now. "You mean when you and Veronica are in California?"

"Here." Mama handed George his camera, pausing to look at him with a funny expression, almost as if she was trying to figure out a problem. Then, just like that, she thanked him and turned away. But it was the look in George's eyes that made Lucy wonder. As he watched Mama going into the house, it almost seemed as if he had a hopeful look in his eyes.

At lunchtime, Lucy carefully watched George and Mama every time they spoke to each other, which wasn't often since Veronica was there and doing most of the talking. But unless it was Lucy's imagination, there seemed to be some kind of invisible conversation going on between Mama and George. It was the way their eyes seemed to light up, the slight lilt in Mama's words, the way George smiled.

As Lucy helped Grandma in the kitchen, she decided to mention it. "Do you think Mama and George are falling in love?" she asked quietly.

Grandma dropped the pan she was scrubbing and turned to stare at Lucy. "What?"

"Do you think—"

"I heard you perfectly fine, Lucy. I just cannot believe you would say such a thing."

"Why?"

Grandma slowly shook her head. "I think you're awfully eager to see someone falling in love. First it was Veronica and George. Now Mama?" Grandma chuckled. "Next thing I know you'll be having George and me falling in love. No, Lucy, I do not think your mama is falling in love with George." Grandma returned to scrubbing the pot.

Lucy wanted to ask Grandma what made her so sure but knew that would only invite more trouble. Besides, Grandma was a grown-up . . . she was probably right.

"Why don't you go visit with Veronica," Grandma suggested as they were finishing up.

Lucy almost admitted to Grandma that she'd rather work in the kitchen, but she knew this would only bring unwanted questions, and when it came to Veronica, Lucy felt more and more confused. As much as she had liked Veronica to start with, she didn't trust the pretty lady too much now.

7

"So, doll, you haven't told me how our little scheme is going,"
Veronica said as Lucy sat down in the chair in the front room.
"Did you manage to convince Georgie that he and I should be
hitting the road tomorrow?"

Lucy felt confused. "But you were at lunch," she reminded
her. "You just heard George telling us that there's too much
snow in the mountains to travel right now."

Veronica scowled. "Yeah . . . but I had hoped you would work
your magic on him."

"My magic?"

Veronica rolled her eyes. "I think you could wrap old Georgie
Porgie right around your little finger."

"Huh?"

Veronica smiled in a way that reminded Lucy of Helen Krausner after she'd said something mean or the way a cat might look
after eating a pretty bird. "Not that it's a bad thing. I happen
to find that to be a rather attractive quality in a man."

"What?" Lucy was hopelessly lost.

"Oh, *never mind!*"

Lucy stood now. It seemed clear her company was not wanted here anymore, but she still needed to remember her manners. "Excuse me, please."

"Wait." Veronica's voice warmed up. "I'm sorry, doll. I suppose I'm in a bit of a snit today, but I shouldn't take it out on you. That's not fair."

Fingering the scratchy fabric of the chair behind her, Lucy waited.

"You see, I'd gotten my hopes up, you know, that George and I would be leaving tomorrow and we'd make Los Angeles by midnight. I even got my bags nearly packed. And now this. I'm severely disappointed."

"Oh . . ."

"But it's not your fault."

There was a long silence with only the sound of the mantel clock ticking, and Lucy was thinking hard. Surely there was some way out of this. Then it hit her. "What about the train in Flagstaff?" she said suddenly. "It might be slow, driving in the snow and all, but I'll bet George could get you that far, Veronica. Then you could get a train ticket and—"

"But what about George?" Veronica's eyes grew wide.

"He could come back here and stay with us until Christmas . . . or until the roads get better." Lucy was smiling now, pleased that she, all by herself, had come up with such a perfect plan. "If you want, I'll even go ask George about this for you. I know where he is and I'm sure he'll—"

"*No.*" Veronica's pale blue eyes turned as frosty as a January morning. "That's not necessary."

"But you could be in Los Angeles soon," Lucy told her. "With all the sunshine and orange trees and Hollywood and everything."

Veronica let out a sad sigh. "Can I tell you a secret, doll?"

Lucy twisted her mouth to one side. On one hand, it was always delicious getting to hear a secret. On the other hand, she felt wary of Veronica. "All right . . ."

"Remember I told you about my bad friend, the one who was taking me to Hollywood to make me a star?"

Lucy nodded. "The man who left you on the highway?"

"Yes. And I told you how he took my money." Veronica held out her hands with palms up. "I am broke."

"Broke?" Lucy thought about Veronica's fine clothes and jewelry and shoes and suitcases. She looked like a rich lady.

"Penniless."

Lucy blinked. "Oh."

"You promised to keep my secret, doll."

Lucy swallowed hard. "So you can't afford to buy a train ticket?"

"No, I can't." She sadly shook her head. "I need George to get me to Hollywood. And since I told you that secret, I might as well tell you another." She peered at Lucy. "Can I trust you?"

"I guess so."

"The truth is, I think George fancies me as much as I fancy him. I think that when we get to California, we will continue getting acquainted, and, well . . ." She giggled. "If George should come to his senses and propose to me, well, I might just forget all about becoming a famous movie actress and star as his wife instead."

"What?" Lucy could not believe her ears.

Veronica shrugged. "I don't know for sure . . . but I might enjoy being married."

Lucy didn't know what to say, and manners or no manners, she suddenly felt the need to get outside and breathe some fresh air. Maybe it was the strong smell of Veronica's flowery perfume or stale fingernail paint or just Veronica herself, but Lucy felt like she was suffocating. Without saying another word, she turned and dashed from the room, grabbed her coat and boots, and, thankful that Grandma wasn't in the kitchen, streaked outside and toward the barn.

The next thing she knew, she was in Mama's arms with tears streaming down her cheeks. "What is it?" Mama demanded as she stroked Lucy's hair. "What happened?"

"Oh, Mama!"

"What? Lucy, please, talk to me. Is it Grandma? Do I need to—"

"No, no, it's not Grandma." Lucy stepped back, wiping her nose with her sleeve right in front of Mama.

"What then?" Mama put a warm hand on Lucy's cheek. "Talk to me."

"It's Veronica," Lucy sputtered. "She—she's going to—to marry George!"

It was almost as if some kind of light went out of Mama's blue eyes. Although she wasn't frowning, her mouth looked sadder than ever, but she simply shook her head. "Oh, Lucy," she said quietly. "Is that what's troubling you?"

"But it's all wrong, Mama. All wrong."

Mama knelt down, looking intently into Lucy's eyes. "It's not your decision to make, Lucy. I know you admire George greatly. But it's not your decision. Everyone has to live their own life. Someday when you're a grown-up you'll understand that better."

"I don't want to be a grown-up," Lucy said stubbornly. "Not ever." She wanted to add that all grown-ups were stupid, but she stopped herself because Mama wasn't stupid. There was no reason to make Mama feel worse. Lucy could tell that she wasn't happy with this news either.

Mama stood, pushing the loose strands of hair away from her flushed face. "Well, someday you will be a grown-up, Lucy. But right now, you're a child. So why don't you go out and play or something?"

"Do you need any help?"

Mama just shook her head, turning back to where she was pegging up a sheet. "Thanks anyway, Lucy. I'm almost done out here."

As Lucy walked back to the house, she decided that Mama was right. Everyone did have to live their own life. She realized that the sooner George and Veronica were able to be on their way, the better it would probably be for everyone.

On Wednesday afternoon, George's big yellow car parked in front of the house, and George came into the front room where Veronica, Grandma, and Lucy were listening to a program on the radio. "Anyone care to go for a ride?" he asked cheerfully.

"I do! I do!" Veronica stood up. "I'll get my coat."

George looked at Grandma and Lucy. "How about you two?"

"Not this time." Grandma stood, making her way toward the kitchen. "I need to get dinner started."

"Lucy?" His brown eyes lit up. "Want to come?"

"No, thank you." She looked down at her lap, picking at the hole in her trousers that was getting bigger.

"Come on, George," Veronica urged as she returned with her fur-trimmed blue coat. "Let's go. I want to go to town. Maybe you can take me to dinner. Or we can go to a movie or—"

"Lucy," George interrupted Veronica, "I thought you might like to drive by and check on Smoky."

Lucy felt her heart lurch. "Smoky?"

"Don't you want to see how he's doing in all this snow?"

She stood and nodded. "Yes. I'll get my coat."

George was waiting outside for Lucy. Veronica was already in the passenger's seat, but George led Lucy to the driver's side. "Slide on into the middle," he told her.

Sitting between George and Veronica, Lucy looked straight forward as George's car headed down the snowy road. She couldn't wait to see Smoky. Usually she stopped and talked to the pony every day on her way home from school. But it had been days since she'd seen him.

"There he is," she said eagerly, pointing to where Smoky was standing beneath the shelter of the trees in the middle of the field. "Do you think he's cold?"

"He's a horse," Veronica said sharply. "He's supposed to be cold."

"He's a pony," Lucy corrected.

"He's probably not too cold," George assured her. "Do you want to get out and say hello?"

"If you don't mind."

"Not at all." George reached behind the seat to pull out a bag, removing a whole apple. "I got these at the store in town. Want to give Smoky one?"

Her eyes grew big. "A whole apple?"

George laughed. "Sure."

"Thanks!"

Before long, Smoky was happily crunching on the apple, and Lucy giggled as his whiskers tickled her palm as he sniffed around for more. "Sorry, Smoky," she told him. "That's all for now."

George held out another apple. "You sure about that?"

"Is it all right?"

"I don't see why not."

Feeling extravagant and happy, she fed Smoky the second apple, petting his head and telling him not to get too cold. "Go on back to your spot by the trees," she said as she climbed down from the fence. "I'll try to come back as soon as I can."

He raised and lowered his head as if he understood. Then George and Lucy headed back to the car, where Veronica was sitting with her arms folded across her front and a slightly sour-looking expression on her face. "Is the horsey happy now?" she asked after George started the car.

"He's a pony," Lucy said. "And yes, he is happy." She turned to George. "So am I. Thank you, George."

"Now that everyone else is happy, do you think we could go to town and have some fun?" Veronica said hopefully.

"We can't stay in town for long," George told her as he drove.

"Why not?" Veronica demanded. "What about taking in a movie? Or dinner?"

"Because we're expected back at the house," George said.

"I need to set the table," Lucy added.

Veronica let out a disgruntled sigh, and Lucy and George exchanged glances.

"I don't know why I even bothered to come then," Veronica said. "I thought we were actually going to have fun."

"I just wanted to take a ride," George told her. "I thought you understood that."

"Then maybe I should ask you to drive me to the train station in Flagstaff," she said in a grumpy tone.

"I'm more than happy to do that," he told her.

She leaned back and made a *humph* sound.

"Would you like me to take you there tomorrow?" George offered.

"No, thank you," she said tersely.

Lucy remembered the secret—that Veronica had no money. Lucy wished she could confide in George. Maybe he could loan Veronica some money, and that would get Veronica on her way . . . and everyone would be happy. But Lucy had promised.

"Why can't you just drive us to Los Angeles?" she asked.

Just then the car slid slightly and George turned the steering wheel, guiding it back to the center of the road. "It should be obvious why I don't want to drive to Los Angeles," he said. "It's slick enough on flat ground. The mountain pass would be treacherous."

"All right." Veronica sat up straighter. "Then we will just have to make the best of it, won't we?"

They were slowly driving through town now, looking at the stores and businesses. Some of them were decorated for Christmas, and with the dusky blue blanket of snow outside, the warm yellow lights coming out of the windows, and the lamplights glowing, it looked like a completely different town.

"It's so pretty," Lucy said slowly. "I never saw town looking so pretty. It's like a picture book."

"Or a Christmas card," George added.

"Look at that sign." Veronica pointed to a poster on a window. "A Christmas dance on Saturday night. Oh, George, can we go? Can we? Can we?"

"I, uh, I don't know."

"Please, George. If we have to be stuck in this little one-horse town, we should at least get to have some fun. Please, say you'll take me to the Christmas dance."

He glanced at Lucy. "Let me think about it."

Using a little girl sort of voice, Veronica begged him a while longer, but George didn't answer one way or another. Even so, all the way home, she continued to chatter on and on about how much fun the dance would be, and what she would wear, and how it would make her time in this "one-horse town" a little more bearable. Lucy wanted to point out that their town had a lot more than just one horse. Although it was possible there was only one pony in Maple Grove. At least only one that Lucy knew about.

By the time they got home, Lucy couldn't wait to get away

from Veronica, but first she spoke politely to George. "It's a very nice car," she told him. "And it was fun to see Smoky today. I know he liked the apples. Thank you very much." Then she hurried into the house and started setting the table.

"We have good news." Grandma set the butter dish on the table.

"What?" Lucy paused with the soup spoons in her hand.

"One more room will be filled starting tomorrow. And for more than a week."

"During Christmastime?"

Grandma explained how the Farleys already had a houseful of people coming to visit. "Their second boy, Howard, is getting married right after Christmas. So Mrs. Farley called to ask if her elderly aunt and uncle could stay here."

"That is good news." Lucy carefully set a soup spoon down.

"Naturally, they'll spend the holidays and whatnot at the Farley house, but we will have them the rest of the time." Grandma smiled as she adjusted a place setting. "Four paying guests during Christmas. It's a real windfall."

Lucy suspected there might not be *four* paying guests. She'd given it some thought, and if Veronica was truly penniless, how would she pay her bill when it came time for her to check out? Not that Lucy planned to mention this to anyone—not after she'd been sworn to secrecy. Even so, Lucy knew that three paying guests were better than none. Unfortunately, it wouldn't be the first time someone had been unable to pay the bill.

8

Mr. and Mrs. Dorchester arrived not long after Lucy and Grandma had cleaned up lunch on Thursday afternoon. "If you're hungry," Lucy said as she showed the older couple to their room, "my grandma will fix you a snack."

"We haven't eaten since breakfast on the train," Mrs. Dorchester said as she set her handbag on the dresser. "And that wasn't anything to speak of. Goodness knows, with the price of train fare these days, one should be able to find something decent to eat on the train."

"Was it exciting traveling by train?" Lucy asked.

"Heavens no!" Mrs. Dorchester unpinned her hat with a sour expression. "I wouldn't wish train travel on my worst enemies."

"Oh." Lucy was surprised since it always looked glamorous in the movies.

"We would've come by automobile except for this horrid snow. Why on earth Howie wanted to get married in the middle of winter is a mystery to me."

"Maybe the bride picked the date," Mr. Dorchester suggested.

She glared at her husband, then looked back at Lucy. "Please tell your grandmother that we would appreciate something to eat as soon as possible," Mrs. Dorchester instructed. "And tell her that I have sensitivity to onions and raw vegetables."

Lucy nodded.

"And if she could please hurry it a bit." Mrs. Dorchester held the back of a plump white hand against her forehead. "I am feeling a bit faint."

"I'll go down and set the table," Lucy told her as she rushed from the room. It seemed like Mrs. Dorchester was going to be what Grandma called a *dingdong fussbudget*. Naturally Grandma hadn't said this knowing that Lucy was listening, and as far as Lucy knew, she'd only said it about that one guest, but Lucy felt certain that Mrs. Dorchester was one of those.

Grandma was warming some leftover stew, which unfortunately had onions that Grandma had tried to pick out, and Lucy was just finishing up the table when George came in, stomping the snow from his boots. "Are you ready to go to town for your Christmas pageant practice?" he asked her.

"Oh, yes!" Lucy looked at the clock. "I nearly forgot."

She set down the last cup and called out to Grandma that George was taking her to town now.

"Did I hear someone say they're going to town?" Veronica said as she came down the stairs. "Any chance I could come along too?"

"We have to get going in the next few minutes," George told her, "in order to get Lucy to the church on time. I'm already warming up the car, so you'd better hurry."

"I won't be but a minute," she chirped as she headed back up the stairs.

Lucy got her coat and things and went outside with George. "Thank you for giving me a ride," she told him.

"It's my pleasure." He grinned as he opened the door for her. "Besides, I need to pick up a little something at Hempley's Garage."

Once they were in the car, she asked how his mechanical work on their old car was coming along. "I haven't told Mama or Grandma anything," she said quietly, as if someone might hear her, although Mama was doing laundry and Grandma was in the kitchen.

"It's coming along just swell," he said. "I expect to have her up and running by Christmas."

"So you *will* stay with us until Christmas?" she said hopefully.

"As long as this weather keeps up, I don't have much of a choice."

She told George about the dingdong fussbudget guest, and he threw back his head and laughed. "They'll be here until after Christmas?"

"Yes, but her husband seems real nice," Lucy assured him. "And I could be wrong about Mrs. Dorchester. Maybe she was just tired. Please don't tell anyone I told you that about her."

"No worries, Lucy. Your secret is safe with me."

Lucy looked back at the house, wondering where Veronica was.

"I told her to hurry," he said. "Maybe we should just leave without her." He put the car into gear, and just as the tires moved, out came Veronica with her coat flapping behind her.

"Wait!" she cried as she hurried down the steps, tugging on her gloves.

The car took off as she closed the car door. "Now I'll need to drive faster than I like," George said.

"I was moving as fast as I could," she told him.

"Remember the reverend said the children aren't to be late." George's car tore through the snow of their driveway and onto the road.

"Well, please excuse me for being a bit slow." Veronica used a sharp-sounding voice. "But if you'd given me a little more notice . . ."

Lucy pressed her lips tightly together and slumped down into the seat. She didn't like to be the reason for their fight, but she couldn't think of anything to say to make things better. The three of them rode in silence, but as they got closer to the Greenburg farm, Lucy sat up tall, hoping to catch a glimpse of Smoky. What she saw sent a cold chill down her spine.

"The sign is gone!" she cried out.

"What sign?" Veronica demanded. "A stop sign? George, do you need to stop?"

"No, not a stop sign." Lucy leaned forward, peering out the windshield, hoping to spy Smoky beneath the trees. "The pony for sale sign."

"Oh, is that all?" Veronica leaned back and chuckled. "I thought for a moment we were going to be in a smash-up."

"I don't see Smoky anywhere," she said to George. "Do you?"

He shook his head. "Can't say that I do, Lucy."

"Do you think someone bought him?" she asked in a small voice.

"Maybe Mr. Greenburg changed his mind about selling him," George suggested.

Lucy just nodded, but deep in the pit of her stomach she didn't think so. No, something told her that Smoky had been sold . . . and taken away.

As a result, she felt less than enthusiastic when she went into the church, where the other children were already up in front getting ready to rehearse. "You're late, Lucy Turnbull," Mrs. Babcock said, frowning.

"I'm sorry," Lucy told her as she peeled off her coat and mittens.

"You can't expect to be late and still have a good part in the pageant," Mrs. Babcock scolded as Lucy went up front to stand with the others. "You asked to be an angel, remember?"

"I really am sorry," Lucy said contritely.

"Never mind." Mrs. Babcock loudly clapped her hands. "I need everyone's attention." She began to instruct them on what they were to do, telling them who was to stand where and when they would come out in front. Lucy tried to pay close attention, but she was distracted by thinking about Smoky. She'd known it was unrealistic to put her hopes on getting a pony for Christmas, but when God had answered her prayers by bringing boarders— and now all the rooms were full—it had seemed like a possibility.

"What's wrong with you?" Helen Krausner asked as the angels were herded to the back of the church to wait for their turn to proceed forward in song. The fact that Helen was playing an angel seemed odd to Lucy. Then again, they were only acting.

Lucy shrugged. "Nothing."

"You look like you just lost your best friend." Helen made a catty smile. "Oh, that's right, you already did."

Lucy frowned at her. "That's not why I'm sad, Helen."

Helen leaned forward, looking slightly concerned. "What is it then? You can tell me."

For whatever reason, maybe just to make her stop asking, Lucy decided to tell. "I'm worried that Mr. Greenburg already sold Smoky, the pony . . . and, well, I was hoping to get him for Christmas." As she said this, she knew how ridiculous she sounded, at least to her own ears, since there was no way Mama could afford a pony. Not that Helen needed to know that. "It was silly, I suppose," she continued. "But I really did like the pony."

"That is very interesting." Helen's eyes twinkled in a mischievous way.

"Why?"

"Because I asked my father to get me that pony for Christmas too."

Lucy felt horrified. "You did?"

Helen nodded. "I have a feeling that is exactly what's happened. Father went out yesterday morning to see about something, and he was gone for most of the day. My mother was not the least bit pleased about it either." Her lips curled into a smug smile. "I'm sure that's what he was doing."

"Girls!" Mrs. Babcock called out. "No talking back there!"

Lucy felt sick inside. It was one thing for Lucy not to become the new owner of Smoky, but it was unbearable to think that someone like Helen was going to have him. Helen didn't even like animals. Lucy remembered the time Helen threw stones at a stray dog. She told everyone that the dog had rabies, but Lucy could tell he was only hungry.

It was time for the angels to march forward singing "Angels We Have Heard on High." Lucy tried to follow along with the words, but her heart was no longer in it.

Lucy was relieved when practice ended and she could make her way to the front door with her coat and mittens in hand.

"Do not forget," Mrs. Babcock called out. "I want you all here on time for Saturday's practice at two in the afternoon. We will have costumes here, and it will be a dress rehearsal."

Lucy nodded and waved, then hurried outside to see that George's yellow roadster was already waiting. She knew she should have enjoyed this moment, being picked up like a princess. She should've taken her time and made sure that Helen Krausner noticed her getting into the fancy car as well as the glamorous Veronica Grant sitting beside her in the front seat. But Lucy felt so downhearted, she didn't even care. As they rode home, she realized she'd completely forgotten to brag about the almost movie star who was staying at their house.

"How did it go?" George asked.

"It was all right," Lucy said glumly.

"After we dropped you off, I thought maybe I should've come inside," Veronica told her.

"Why?" Lucy turned to look at her.

"To help with the acting."

"Oh." Lucy nodded. "Maybe you can help on Saturday."

Veronica began to talk about some of the acting she'd done

back in St. Louis, and how she couldn't wait to get to Hollywood and try it out again, and on and on and on. Lucy resisted the urge to cover her ears with her hands. Instead, she leaned back into the seat and closed her eyes, trying hard not to think about anything. Unfortunately, all she could think about was that Helen Krausner was going to have her pony!

Lucy got both George and Veronica's word that they would not mention the pony to Mama. "It will only make her feel bad," Lucy told them as they neared home. "We couldn't afford a pony anyway. And Mama told me she didn't want me putting my hopes into something that was impossible. No sense in telling her about it now."

"You can trust me with your secret," Veronica assured her as George parked in front of the house. She winked like this was a fun game, then hopped out of the car and hurried up to the house, as the snow was coming down hard again.

George helped Lucy out of the car. Once they were on the porch he leaned over, placing a hand on her shoulder. "You know you can trust me too, Lucy. I just hope you're not too terribly disappointed."

"It's probably for the best," she told him. "Ponies are for rich people. Mama said it was like wishing for the moon." Of course, that was not how Lucy felt. But she'd learned long ago . . . maybe when Daddy died . . . that you didn't usually get what you wished for. She should've known better than to wish for a pony.

With more guests in the house, including the dingdong fussbudget and the rather spoiled almost-actress, life became noisier and busier than ever. Lucy didn't mind the extra activity and responsibilities, though, because it took her mind off of Smoky. Before bed, she removed the picture she'd drawn from her wall, tucking it into the bottom of a drawer. If Mama noticed as Lucy said her prayers, she didn't mention it.

As usual, of late anyway, some of the grown-ups stayed up in the front room talking. Sometimes Lucy tried to understand their words, but she was just far enough away that although she could make out who was speaking, she couldn't quite make out what they were saying. Tonight it was all four of their guests and Mama. Grandma must have gone to bed already.

After a while the Dorchesters made their way upstairs, leaving just George and Veronica . . . and Mama. Lucy was surprised that Mama was staying up so late, but from the gay sound of their voices, they were enjoying each other's company. Naturally, that made Lucy curious. Despite knowing that Mama would not approve, Lucy sneaked out of bed and down the hallway to where she could hear them plainly.

"I'm sure you'll make a fine movie actress," Mama was saying. "I honestly hope to see you in our little theater someday."

"Oh, do go on," Veronica crooned.

"You're very beautiful," Mama continued. "My own daughter told my mother that she thinks you're the most beautiful person she's ever laid eyes on."

"But surely she thinks you're beautiful too," Veronica said. "All little girls think their mothers are beautiful."

Mama laughed, but it didn't sound like a real laugh.

"Of course Lucy thinks Miriam is beautiful," George said. "Anyone can see that just to look at her."

"To look at whom?" Veronica asked.

"Miriam, of course." George chuckled. "Wouldn't you agree that she's a beautiful woman?"

"Oh, I wouldn't—"

"I was talking to Veronica." George cut Mama off. "You consider yourself an expert on beauty, Veronica. Look at Miriam's fine skin, those topaz blue eyes, her straight nose and—"

"That's enough," Mama said in a voice that Lucy didn't recognize. Was she mad, or embarrassed, or something else? "If you will excuse me, I would like to—"

"I'm sorry, Miriam," George said gently. "I didn't mean to offend you. But you were so complimentary to Veronica, it seemed only right that—"

"No apology needed," Mama said crisply. "Now if you will excuse me, I need to tend to some things in the kitchen for breakfast."

"Yes, we should all call it a night," George said. There was the sound of movement, and Lucy scampered like a mouse back to her room, leaping into her bed and pulling the covers up to her chin, worried that Mama might check on her. But after a bit, once her breathing evened out, Lucy heard talking again. This time it came from the kitchen and was only the sound of George and Mama's voices. Once again, Lucy tiptoed out to listen.

"I really am sorry," George was saying. "I know I made you uncomfortable, and that wasn't my goal at all."

"Never mind," Mama told him.

"I only wanted to put Veronica in her place," he said. "She sets such high stock on appearances, and she spends so much time worrying about her own. Yet you go about your business, you take care of everyone and everything, and in my opinion you are much more beautiful than Veronica. Not in a painted flashy way, of course, but in a lovely womanly way. I just hope you don't mind me saying so."

"Thank you, George." Mama's voice sounded stiff as the stove door clanked closed.

"I can tell I've offended you now."

"No . . . I'm not offended. Just uncomfortable."

"I suppose I've stuck my foot in my mouth again. Sometimes that got me into trouble at law school. On the other hand, I think a good lawyer knows how to speak his mind, even if no one else wants to hear the truth."

"I suppose the truth . . . like beauty . . . can be in the eye of the beholder."

He chuckled.

"Now, really, George, if you will excuse me, it's getting late."

"I will excuse you only if you promise that you'll forgive me for offending you."

"You did not offend me."

The kitchen was quiet for what felt like several minutes.

"Good night, George." Mama's voice sounded just a tiny bit more gentle, and now her footsteps were coming Lucy's way.

"Good night, Miriam," George called. Lucy was already making a beeline for her bed again. This time she stayed put. But what she heard in the kitchen did get her mind to wondering. Now that she knew she wasn't getting a pony for Christmas, maybe she should consider praying for something else—like a daddy!

9

After lunch on Friday, George invited Lucy to take a ride in his car, but once she was inside, he told her his real purpose. "Your house needs a Christmas tree," he said as the car took off over the snowy road. "You and I are going to find the perfect one."

As they drove, they talked. Mostly it seemed that George wanted to know more about Mama, and since Lucy thought she knew why he wanted to know more, she was happy to oblige him. Unfortunately, his questions only revealed that she did not know as much about her mother as she thought she did. Oh, she knew that Mama liked birds and growing flowers in the springtime. She knew that Mama was a good cook but that it made Grandma feel important to handle the cooking, so she stayed out of the kitchen most of the time. She knew that Mama took care of the laundry and sewing and some of the housekeeping and most of the outdoor chores and that Mama was kind and good and sometimes stern. Finally she thought of something she hadn't told him.

"Mama used to have the prettiest smile," she said as he parked the car near a grove of ponderosa pine trees. "But after Daddy died, it just seemed to go away."

"That's understandable."

"I prayed that God would give Mama her smile back," Lucy confessed as they got out of the car. "For Christmas."

George had a real thoughtful look as he reached for his pipe. "Maybe God's going to answer that prayer for you."

"You know what?" She felt a rush of excitement.

"What?"

"I'd rather have Mama's smile back than a pony."

George looked shocked. "No kidding?"

"It's true." She nodded eagerly.

That night the Christmas tree, which reached clear to the ceiling, was in place. "I've never seen a Christmas tree quite like this one." George touched a long-needled bough. "But I think it might be the most beautiful tree ever."

"It's certainly the biggest tree this house has ever seen," Mama told him.

"It didn't look that tall in the woods."

She shook her head. "I know I won't have enough ornaments to fill it."

"We can make some more," Lucy suggested.

"We can string popcorn," Grandma told her.

"Yes!" Lucy exclaimed. "Let's do that now."

"Not tonight, we won't," Mama said. "It's already past Lucy's bedtime."

Lucy groaned.

"We'll do it tomorrow night," Mama said gently.

"That reminds me," Veronica said suddenly. "Tomorrow night is the Christmas dance. Remember, George? You promised to take me."

"What?" George frowned. "I don't recall making—"

"Remember, we saw the poster in town," she reminded him.

"George didn't promise," Lucy pointed out. "He only said he'd think about it."

"Oh, please, George," Veronica pleaded. "Take me to the Christmas dance, I'm begging you. *Please*."

"That must be the grange dance," Grandma said. "They have it every year."

"I remember hearing about a Christmas dance up north somewhere, in a barn as I recall," Mrs. Dorchester said. "Horrible tale about how the whole place caught on fire and everyone was trapped inside. Nearly half the town was burned to death, and just before Christmas."

"Oh, dear!" Mama's brows lifted.

"Good heavens!" Grandma let out a loud sigh that sounded like *fussbudget* to Lucy's ears.

"Well, that's silly," Veronica told her. "People don't die at dances."

"Just the same, you won't catch us going to any Christmas dance at a grange." Mrs. Dorchester grimly shook her head.

"No, sirree. Now, come on, Fred, it's time you and I turned in for the night. My back is starting to ache something fierce."

"Time for me to call it a day too," Grandma said. "I'll say my good-nights now."

"And so will Lucy." Mama put a hand on Lucy's shoulder, guiding her out.

"Good night, everyone, sleep tight," Lucy called out, refraining from adding "don't let the bedbugs bite" like she sometimes did, since she knew Mama wouldn't approve. Not with paying guests in the house.

It wasn't until Lucy had finished quickly saying her prayers and was tucked snugly in bed that she knew she had to say something before it was too late. "You can't let Veronica talk George into taking her to that dance," she proclaimed just as Mama pulled the string on the overhead light.

"What?" Mama stood in the doorway, her silhouette framed in light.

"Veronica will just keep pestering George," Lucy explained. "And he's so nice, he might give in."

"Give in to what?"

"You know what, Mama. He'll take her to that dance."

Now Mama came back in, closing the door behind her and sitting down in the chair again. "What difference would that make, Lucy?" Her voice was soft and quiet in the darkness.

"The difference would be that George is falling in love with you."

Mama laughed in an odd way. "Oh, Lucy, your imagination is running away—"

"It's not my imagination. It's true."

"How do you know it's true?" Mama was whispering now, as if worried that someone might be listening.

"Because he kept asking about you when we got the tree." Lucy thought for a moment, trying to recall if George had asked her not to mention this, but she couldn't remember anything quite like that.

"What was he asking?"

"Just *stuff*, Mama." Lucy felt anxious. "But you can't waste time. You need to go out there and make sure Veronica doesn't talk him into it. She can be awfully persistent when she wants something."

"So I've noticed."

"Please, Mama. You have to trust me on this."

Mama slowly stood. "I can't make any promises, Lucy."

"Just try. *Please*."

"Good night, Lucy." Mama opened the door again. "I love you."

"I love you too, Mama—now hurry!"

Lucy could hear the sound of their voices in the living room, and to her surprise it all sounded quite pleasant again. There was even laughter. Then, just as she was considering sneaking out of bed again, it sounded as if they were all saying good night. This was followed by the sounds of footsteps and doors closing, and Lucy knew that everyone had gone to bed and she'd have to wait until morning to find out how it went. Hopefully Mama had managed to prevent what could be a disaster from happening.

On Saturday morning, Lucy was surprised by two things. First of all, she was surprised that Veronica was up in time to sit with them at breakfast. Dressed in an elegant green blouse and matching trousers, Veronica seemed fully awake and more intent than usual on keeping and maintaining George's attention. The second surprise was discovering that George had pulled a fast one last night.

"George told me that the only way he'll take me to the Christmas dance tonight is if Miriam goes too," Veronica announced. "I'm not sure if he thinks we need a chaperone or if he just wants to walk in with two women on his arm, but he made it clear that it's the only way he'll go." She turned to Mama, and Lucy waited hopefully. "You promised to sleep on it, Miriam. Have you made up your mind?"

Mama placed her napkin in her lap. "I'm afraid I have to decline."

"Oh, Miriam." Veronica pursed her lips together.

"Why, Mama?" Lucy asked. "You should go to the dance and have fun."

"I agree," Grandma said. "You should go to the dance. It's been years since you've been to a dance." She gave George a sly look. "Miriam used to be one of the best dancers in these parts."

"Oh, Mother."

"Is that true, Mama?" Lucy asked eagerly.

"No, of course not. Your grandmother is exaggerating."

Grandma shook her finger. "It is so true." She winked at Lucy. "Your mama and daddy used to go to the grange dances, back before you were born, and the word around town was that those two could really cut the rug." She laughed.

"Then you really should go to the dance," George urged her.

"Yes," Lucy chimed in. "Say you'll go."

"But I . . . I don't know." Mama slowly shook her head.

"Come on, Miriam," Veronica urged with a bit less enthusiasm. "Just do it for me. I've been so bored, and a dance sounds like such fun."

"Come on, Mama," Lucy tried. "Just go with them."

"You might enjoy the music," George added.

"And the dancing." Grandma grinned at her.

"Unless the whole place goes up in flames." Mrs. Dorchester grimaced as she reached for a second helping of fried potatoes. She must not have noticed the onions Grandma put in them.

Mama looked caught now. "Well, I suppose it wouldn't hurt to go."

"Of course it wouldn't hurt." Grandma cut off a piece of butter.

"Unless you all burned up."

Mama looked directly at Mrs. Dorchester now. "I really don't think that's a possibility. The grange has been having dances since I was a girl, and I've never had any reason to worry."

"Then come to the dance," George said happily.

It seemed settled. As odd as it was, Mama and George and Veronica were all going to the dance together. Lucy wondered if he would take turns dancing with them or attempt to dance with two partners at the same time.

After breakfast, alone with Mama and Grandma in the kitchen, Lucy asked Mama what she was going to wear.

"Oh, I don't know." Mama scrubbed a dish. "My Sunday dress, I suppose."

"What about that pretty blue shiny dress," Lucy said. "The one in the back of your closet. You never wear it."

"The topaz silk," Grandma said. "You should wear that, Miriam."

"I doubt it will even fit." Mama wiped her damp hands on the front of her stained apron and frowned.

"I don't see why it won't fit," Grandma told her. "And if we need to, we could make some alterations."

"But why go to such trouble?"

"Lucy?" called Veronica from the dining room. "Are you busy, doll?"

"Why don't you go see what she wants," Grandma said. "We'll finish up in here."

Lucy removed her apron and went to see.

"I nearly forgot that I made a promise to you."

"A promise?" Lucy followed her into the front room.

"I told you we'd go to the movie theater on Saturday. Your mother even agreed to it. Remember how I wanted to go last Sunday, and she said that was unacceptable?" One of Veronica's thin eyebrows arched higher. "So . . . what do you think, doll? Do you want to see a picture with me or not?"

Lucy felt a rush of excitement at this unexpected offer. "You mean it?"

"Of course. In light of your disappointment over that horse

yesterday, it seems like a good idea. You need a little pick-me-up." Veronica ran her hand over Lucy's hair.

"How will we get there?"

"George said he'd be happy to take us if you want to go. I told him I was absolutely certain you'd want to go. You do, don't you?" Veronica smiled hopefully. "I'm just dying to see a picture today."

Suddenly Lucy remembered today's Christmas pageant rehearsal. Disappointment seeped in as she reminded Veronica that she had to be at the church by two. "Maybe it's not such a good idea after all."

Veronica waved her hand. "Oh, don't you worry about that, doll. We'll go to the early matinee, and you'll be out in plenty of time to make it to your dress rehearsal. The church is only a couple of blocks from the theater. If George isn't back by then, we'll just walk over."

"George doesn't want to go to the picture with us?" Lucy asked.

"Not this time, doll. He says he has something he's working on." She rolled her eyes. "I told him that all work and no play makes George a dull boy, but he didn't seem to care."

"At least he's taking you and Mama to the Christmas dance," Lucy pointed out.

"Yes. This is going to be a red-letter day. Now you go and get yourself dolled up, and I'll speak to your mother about our plans."

Lucy was a little unsure about this but decided not to protest. By the time she emerged, dressed in her best school dress with ribbons tied on her braids, Veronica seemed to have smoothed everything over with Mama just fine. "Just be sure and mind your manners," Mama told her. "And don't be late for pageant practice. You know how Mrs. Babcock can be."

"Yes, Mama." Lucy blew her a kiss as they went out, and soon they were on the road. Today Lucy tried not to look at Mr. Greenburg's farm, but she did notice the sign was still gone. It wasn't long until George was dropping them in front of the movie theater and her sadness was replaced with anticipation as she followed Veronica to the ticket booth.

As she waited, she felt concerned. Hadn't Veronica said she was penniless? And didn't it cost a nickel to see a motion picture? Just the same, Lucy stood back, watching as Veronica consulted with the man in the booth. Lucy could tell by his expression that he was quite taken by Veronica Grant's exotic beauty. Perhaps he thought she was a film star and would let them in for free.

"The movie doesn't start for a while," Veronica explained. "Do you want to walk around town for a bit? Maybe we could get some soda or an ice cream."

Lucy wasn't going to argue with that plan either, although she wondered how they would pay for such things if Veronica was truly broke. But she watched with wide eyes as Veronica extracted a dollar bill from her shiny black purse. Lucy gratefully thanked her, feeling like she was someone else, or starring in a movie, as she strolled through town with Veronica Grant, sipping on her cherry soda. When they stood in line at the theater, she felt people watching them curiously, probably wondering who this elegant person was and why she was here. Lucy just smiled to herself, wishing that Helen Krausner was around to see them together but knowing she would hear all about it eventually. Word traveled fast in their town.

The movie playing was called *Beg, Borrow or Steal*, and it was unlike any other film that Lucy had ever seen. A bunch of men made a business of lying and tricking everyone in order to get money. The actress in it, a blonde lady playing Joyce, was very nice and her clothes were pretty. Still, Lucy was disappointed that Shirley Temple wasn't in it as well. That would have made it lots better. Lucy supposed it was a grown-up movie, and there were a number of parts she didn't quite understand. However, she was amazed at the ending of the movie by Joyce's wedding dress. It was the most beautiful gown Lucy had ever seen. Unfortunately, Joyce was about to marry the wrong man. But the good guy (who also turned out to be a wealthy count) showed up at the right time, and Joyce married him instead. Whew!

"Did you like it, doll?" Veronica asked as they went out into the bright daylight where the sunshine shimmered on the brilliant white snow.

"Yes." Lucy blinked. "Thank you for taking me, Veronica." She almost questioned Veronica about being "broke" but decided not to say that because it sounded ungrateful. Perhaps Veronica had gone to a bank or something. She knew that grown-ups sometimes went there to get money, although Mama had told Lucy they couldn't do that anymore. "Do you know what time it is? I don't want to be late for rehearsal."

Veronica looked at the watch George had loaned her to keep track of the time. "Oh dear, I completely forgot about that. We'd better hurry." She took Lucy by the hand and partly walked and partly ran down the boardwalk toward the church. "Now remember, Lucy, the best part of acting happens *inside* of you. You must think that you are an angel, and then you will act like one."

Lucy laughed. "I don't think I'm much of an angel."

When they reached the church steps, Veronica paused to catch her breath. "Here we are!" she puffed. "Now go—and be the most beautiful angel, doll."

"Do you want to come in?" Lucy asked hopefully.

"Not this time." Veronica patted her hair. "I think I'll call George to come pick me up. It's time for my afternoon nap."

"I better go in." Lucy grabbed the door handle, hoping she wasn't late. But once inside the church, she saw that the other children were already wearing their costumes and getting in their places, and Mrs. Babcock did not look the least bit pleased to see her.

"Lucy Turnbull, you are *twenty minutes* late," she scolded. "I've given your part of an angel to Molly Price. Now you will have to be a sheep." She pointed to a heap of wooly sheep-colored blankets, just like Lucy had worn when she played a sheep last year. "Hurry and get ready now." Mrs. Babcock clapped her hands to get everyone's attention.

Feeling a mixture of shame and deep disappointment, Lucy picked up a grayish and slightly musty-smelling blanket and threw it over her head and back like a cape. With burning cheeks and teary eyes, she walked over to join the other sheep, three slightly unruly boys who didn't even want to be in the pageant.

Knowing that she probably deserved this punishment, she got down on her hands and knees with the snickering boys, and hanging her head low, she wondered how she would explain this to Mama.

After practice ended, Helen Krausner came over to Lucy. "That's just terrible that you have to be a sheep again this year. It's so much more glamorous playing an angel. The angel costumes are even prettier this year than last year."

Lucy didn't know what to say, but she was determined not to let Helen make her feel any worse than she already felt. "Well, they can't be as glamorous as the movie actress who's staying at our house."

Helen looked doubtful. "You have a movie actress staying at your house?"

"Well, she's not a star yet, but she's on her way to Hollywood. Her name is Veronica Grant, and the reason I'm late is because she took me to see *Beg, Borrow or Steal* at the theater today."

"You saw *that* movie?"

Lucy nodded. "With Veronica. Wait until you see her, Helen. Veronica Grant is the most glamorous person that's ever been in Maple Grove."

"When will I see her?" Helen demanded.

Lucy thought. "Well, if you're in church tomorrow."

"I don't know about church." Helen frowned. "My father doesn't want to go . . . sometimes."

"Oh . . ." Lucy nodded, trying to figure this out.

"But at the pageant, for sure."

"I promise to introduce you to her."

111

"She's really going to be an actress?"

Lucy nodded eagerly. "I think she'll be really good too."

As the girls parted ways, Lucy wondered why she'd gone to such efforts to impress someone like Helen Krausner. Really, what did it matter what Helen thought?

10

Y ou're being awfully quiet," George said. Long blue shadows
   cut into the white snow as he drove Lucy away from town
after the dress rehearsal. "Anything wrong?"

Lucy felt her chin trembling as she shook her head no.

He gave her a concerned look. "You sure about that?"

She bit into her lower lip, feeling hot tears burning in her
eyes. But she was determined not to cry.

"Did something bad happen today? At the movies? Or at
pageant practice?"

The caring tone in his voice broke her, and suddenly she was
sobbing. George pulled the car over to the side of the road, right
next to Clara's old house, which looked even sadder and lonelier
in this dusky blue light. George reached into his pocket, then
handed her a handkerchief. "Want to talk about it?"

She wiped her eyes and nose and slowly nodded. Then, as if
someone had popped the cork off a bottle, it all came pouring

out—how she'd been late and demoted from an angel to a sheep. "The sheep are the worst roles to get in the whole pageant."

George reached over and patted her on the shoulder. "I'm sorry," he told her. "Is there anything I can do? I'd be happy to go explain to Mrs. Babcock that it's not your fault and—"

"No," she said quickly. "It's too late to fix it."

He slowly nodded, rubbing his chin like he was thinking. "You know the real reason we celebrate Christmas, don't you? I mean, beyond Santa Claus and jingle bells and Christmas trees?"

"You mean because Jesus was born?" she asked.

"Yes . . . but did you ever think about *how* Jesus was born? I mean, have you considered how it was such a humble birth, in a small barn . . . how he was laid in a hay trough . . . how the Son of almighty God humbled himself to be born in such lowly conditions? Have you thought about it like that?"

She shrugged, unsure of what George was trying to say. Of course she knew all about the stable and the manger. Wasn't she playing a sheep in the pageant?

"Jesus could've been born in a fine palace, Lucy. After all, he was the Son of God. But for some reason God chose humble beginnings for his Son. Do you ever wonder why?"

Lucy shook her head.

"I think it's because God wanted to show that his love could reach to everyone, no matter who they were, from the poorest of poor to great kings. Remember the three wise men who brought treasures to Jesus?"

She nodded. "Some of the older boys are playing the wise men. They're singing the three kings song."

114

"Here is what I'm thinking, Lucy. You getting to play the lowliest of animals is a little bit like Jesus must have felt by getting to be born in a stable."

She tilted her head to one side as she thought about this.

"Not only that, but do you know what animal Jesus is sometimes called?"

"An animal?" She frowned. Surely no nice person would call Jesus an animal.

"He was called the Lamb of God, Lucy."

"Oh . . . yeah . . . I do remember that now."

"If Jesus, the King of Kings, was called the Lamb of God, maybe it's not so bad being a sheep in the Christmas pageant . . . don't you think?"

"I'm not sure, George. The truth is, I still want to be an angel." She forced a little smile. "But that does make me feel better."

He grinned. "Good. Now we'd better get home. Your mother said dinner will be early tonight in order for us to get to the Christmas dance on time."

"The Christmas dance!" she exclaimed. "I completely forgot about that." The sky was dusky periwinkle now. "You better hurry, George!"

The house seemed busier than ever when Lucy went inside. Mr. and Mrs. Dorchester were sitting on the couch as a radio program with Christmas music played loudly. Veronica was all dressed up in a shiny red gown which seemed to match her painted nails and lips. Lucy blinked to see how low it was cut, both in the front and in the back. Wouldn't she get cold in it? However, her cheeks looked more flushed than usual as she danced around the front room as if to entertain the elderly guests.

"You look beautiful," Lucy paused to tell Veronica. "Like a real movie star."

"Thank you, doll." Veronica rewarded her with a flashy smile. "I feel like a real movie star tonight."

Lucy excused herself as she rushed toward the dining room where Mama was placing food on the already set table. "Sorry I'm late," she told Mama.

"That's all right. Hang up your coat and see if Grandma needs help in there. We're eating early tonight because—"

"I know," Lucy called as she pushed through the swinging door. "George told me all about it."

"There you are," Grandma said with a flushed face. "How was the motion picture, Lucy?"

"It was wonderful." Lucy peeled off her coat. "Well, maybe not exactly *wonderful*, but I did enjoy it."

"Here," Grandma set a bowl of cream on the table, handing Lucy the eggbeater. "Can you whip this for me?"

"Sure."

"What was the title of the picture you saw?"

"*Beg, Borrow or Steal,*" Lucy told her. Then as she turned the handle on the beater, trying to keep it balanced on the bottom of the slippery bowl, she told Grandma a bit about the movie.

"Goodness," Grandma said. "It sounds like a bunch of crooks and tricksters to me."

"They weren't all bad," Lucy said defensively. "The father learned his lesson by the end of the movie. And the wedding was absolutely beautiful." As she was describing the gown, Mama came in.

"Speaking of gowns . . ." Grandma frowned at Mama. "Why aren't you dressed for the dance by now? Veronica is out there parading around in her fancy finery."

Mama sighed as she held out the skirt of her stained apron. "Because I'm still working. Why would I want to take the chance of soiling my silk dress?"

"That's what aprons are for." Grandma handed her a bowl of green beans.

"Oh, Mother, that blue silk is not the kind of dress one wears an apron with."

"Did you try it on?" Lucy asked eagerly. "Did it fit right and look pretty?"

"I had to make some alterations," Mama told her, "but I think it will be just fine, Lucy."

Soon it was dinnertime, and it seemed everyone had something to talk about. Mrs. Dorchester had spent the afternoon helping with wedding preparations at the Farleys', which, according to her, were frivolous nonsense. "I did enjoy seeing my niece, but why she wants to make such fussy little decorations is beyond me."

Veronica began to tell about the wedding scene in the movie, describing in detail the preparations for that lavish wedding. "Of course, these were very wealthy people," she said, "not just simple farm folks."

Lucy wanted to point out that they weren't as wealthy as they were pretending to be and that their wealth was wrongfully gained, but by then Veronica was so caught up in describing the bride's costume that Lucy couldn't help but listen.

"It really was beautiful," Lucy told them. "She looked like a fairy princess."

"Someday I'd like to have a wedding like that." Veronica looked longingly at George, as if she wanted him to participate in it.

"I'm sure that all girls dream of weddings," he said. He tipped his head to Lucy. "How about you? Do you dream of a wedding?"

Lucy giggled and looked down at her plate.

The conversation continued, moving faster than usual, and Lucy felt lost through most of it. That was because she was still trying not to feel bad over losing her part as an angel . . . and trying to decide when it would be best to tell Mama. Before she knew it dinner was over, it was time to clean up, Mama went off to get dressed for the Christmas dance, and Lucy was carrying dishes to the kitchen.

She was just starting to dry dishes when Mama came into the kitchen. Lucy almost dropped the saucer in her hand as she stared at the woman in the silky blue dress. "Mama, is that really you?"

Mama laughed as she did a little turn that made the skirt swirl out at the bottom. Lucy dried her hands and went closer to see better. Mama's light brown hair was piled higher than usual on her head, and holding it in place was a shiny pin with white and blue jewels. "Are those real diamonds?" Lucy asked in wonder.

"No, of course not. They're rhinestones."

"And that pin?" Lucy pointed to the smooth white brooch on the front of Mama's dress.

"That was mine," Grandma said proudly. "Your grandfather gave that to me on our wedding day. It's a moonstone."

"A moonstone," Lucy said slowly. "It does remind me of a moon." She threw her arms around Mama. "Oh, Mama, you are beautiful."

Mama smiled down at Lucy—*really smiled*—and Lucy thought her heart was going to burst just to see that smile. "Thank you, Lucy."

"You are the most beautiful lady in the whole world," Lucy told her.

Mama's smile got bigger. "You don't think my shoes look a bit silly with this dress?" She held out a foot.

"Those are your good Sunday shoes," Lucy reminded her. "I think they look just fine."

"So do I!" Grandma reached over and pinched Mama's cheeks.

"What are you doing?" Lucy asked.

"Just giving her a bit of color."

Lucy laughed. "I think she's already got lots of color."

Mama glanced at the kitchen clock. "Well, I feel a little nervous about this, but I suppose I should go out and tell them I'm ready."

"I'll get your good coat and your black leather gloves for you," Lucy offered.

"And my wool scarf," Mama said. "It will be cold tonight."

When Lucy joined the others in the front room, Veronica already had on her fur-trimmed coat and was looking at Mama with a curious expression. However, it was George's face that really got Lucy's attention. His eyes were fastened on Mama, and his mouth was smiling. "Here you go, Mama." Lucy started to hand Mama her things.

"Let me help with that," George offered as he reached to take Mama's black coat. Lucy waited as he helped Mama into it.

Feeling more happy than she had imagined possible considering all that had gone wrong in her life recently, Lucy handed Mama her gloves and scarf. "I hope you have a real fun time at the dance tonight."

"Oh, I'm sure I will," Mama told her. "Now don't you stay up late, you hear?"

Lucy nodded obediently, and just like that, they were off. Lucy wondered what their evening would be like. Judging by the look in Veronica's eye, it would be interesting at least. Hopefully Mama would tell Grandma about it in detail . . . and Lucy would be close enough to listen.

True to her promise, Lucy went to bed on time. Grandma walked her to her bedroom and offered to help her get ready for bed, but Lucy could tell she was tired. "That's all right." She hugged her tightly. "I'm a big enough girl to get myself to bed. I just let Mama help me because she likes to so much."

Grandma chuckled as she gently tugged one of Lucy's braids. "I just hope your mama is having a good time tonight."

"Me too." Lucy sat down to unlace her shoes. She wanted to ask Grandma if she thought George was in love with Mama, but she remembered how Grandma had responded to that last time. Besides, Grandma hadn't been in the front room to see how George's eyes had lit up when he was looking at Mama in her fine blue dress.

"Good night, Lucy." Grandma bent down to kiss her cheek.

"Good night." Lucy pulled off a shoe. "Sleep tight and don't let the bedbugs bite."

"Lucy!" Grandma put a forefinger over her lips. "Don't let the guests hear you saying that."

Lucy giggled. "Sorry. Good night, Grandma."

"You will say your prayers, won't you?"

Lucy nodded . . . but in her heart, she wasn't so sure. What if God was mad at her for being late to practice and then not telling Mama about it? Despite George's encouragement, Lucy felt worried. By the time she was in her nightgown, her feet were cold as ice, so she hopped into bed and tried not to think about anything at all. Not angels or sheep or even ponies. But Mama's sweet smile stayed fixed in her memory, and if she'd been of a mind to pray, she would've prayed that Mama and George were having a really great time at the dance and that they would fall truly in love with each other. As it was, she felt too guilty—and sleepy—to pray at all.

To Lucy's surprise, Veronica made an appearance at the breakfast table on Sunday. But something told Lucy that she was not in a very happy mood. For that matter, neither were George or Mama. In fact, everyone seemed quiet and subdued, especially after the joviality of their last meal together. In between feeding chickens and filling the wood box, Lucy spent much of the morning trying to pin down Mama in regard to last night's festivities, but Mama had been tight-lipped and something else too. Lucy thought perhaps Mama was *distracted*. That's what Mama said about Lucy sometimes, when her mind was somewhere else. Before she could get to the bottom of it, it was time to go to church.

As usual, the Brewsters stopped by to offer a ride. George also planned to drive. However, his roadster only had one seat, so Grandma and the Dorchesters decided to go with the Brewsters, and Mama was about to join them when George stepped in.

"Why don't you ride with me, Miriam?" he said cheerfully.

Mama looked somewhat surprised but pleased. "Well, I suppose—"

"But there won't be room in the roadster," Veronica said quickly. "Not if Lucy is coming with us, George."

Now Lucy stepped back. As much as she liked riding in George's nice car, she wanted Mama to ride with him. "I'll ride in the Brewsters' rumble seat," she said. "That's fun."

"But it's so cold," Mama told her.

"That's all right." Lucy smiled as she moved toward the Brewsters' car. "I don't mind. I just pretend it's a sleigh ride." Satisfied that she'd secured Mama a snug spot next to George, Lucy waited for Mr. Brewster to open the rumble seat. But as she got into the outdoor seat, she noticed Veronica's feathered hat ducking into George's car, and then Veronica slid to the center of the seat so that Mama had to sit by the door. Still,

Mama seemed fine, holding her head high as George headed the big yellow car down the snowy lane.

Lucy tried not to fume at Veronica as they rode to church. It was bad enough that she hadn't said her prayers last night, but to go to church angry . . . well, that just didn't seem right. Especially on the Sunday before Christmas.

The Brewsters' car pulled up by the church just as George was hopping out of his parked car. Lucy watched as George ran around to the passenger side and, with a flourish and a bow, opened the door, offered Mama his hand, and helped her out of the car. Completely ignoring Veronica, George led Mama up the church steps.

Lucy restrained herself from letting out a victory whoop as Mr. Brewster parked directly behind the yellow roadster, but she couldn't help but feel this meant that George was choosing Mama over Veronica. Feeling just a little sorry for Veronica as she crawled out of the car, adjusting the shiny purple feather on her hat, Lucy jumped down out of the rumble seat, made a sprint toward Veronica, and took her by the hand. "Did you have a nice ride?" she asked as they walked together into church.

Veronica made a stiff smile, holding her coat closed against the wind. "It's colder than the dickens today. I don't know how you could stand riding in that rumble seat, doll."

"It wasn't so bad." Even so, Lucy shivered as they went inside.

"Oh, to be in California," Veronica said dramatically.

Lucy nodded as if she agreed—and in truth, she did. If a genie appeared right now, offering her one magic wish today, she would ask that Veronica be whisked off to California immediately, or at least before sunset. (Or else she would do the smart thing and wish for three more wishes!) But as the congregation began to sing, Lucy realized that daydreaming about genies and wishes probably wasn't the best use of one's time during church. When it was time to silently bow her head before God, Lucy told him that she was sorry about being late for pageant practice and promised to tell Mama the truth at her first opportunity. After that, singing the hymns and Christmas songs felt so much better. Lucy felt certain she'd be able to say her bedtime prayers properly tonight. At least she hoped so.

11

The rest of Sunday passed in a flurry that started when Mrs. Dorchester tripped while going up the stairs shortly after their midday meal. It took Mama, Grandma, and Mr. Dorchester to get her safely down the stairs and onto the front room sofa, and the whole time she was howling in pain. Mama called Dr. Mickelson, who came by to see what could be done.

"It looks like a bad ankle sprain," he proclaimed. "Best thing you can do is to stay off of it for a couple of weeks."

"How am I supposed to do that?" she sputtered. "There's my nephew's wedding to attend to, and then I need to get home, and good grief, our room is up those doggone stairs." She pointed to the staircase as if it were to blame for her clumsiness.

Dr. Mickelson shrugged as he wiped the lenses of his glasses. "I'll have someone drop some crutches and other things by." He wrote something down in a little black book. "I've got something in my satchel for your pain." He glanced over at the stairs. "But you won't be going up those stairs for some time." He turned to Mama. "Is there a room down here that she can use?"

Mama frowned. "There are only two rooms down here. My mother and I share one, and Lucy is in the—"

"She can have my room," Lucy offered.

So it was that George spent a couple of hours helping Lucy to switch things from her room and the bedroom upstairs. It took lots of trips up and down the stairs, but George never complained once. Meanwhile Mama did her best to make Mrs. Dorchester comfortable and happy . . . which was not easy. Grandma tended to her usual chores in the kitchen.

Shortly before dinnertime, everything was set. Lucy was settled in the middle room upstairs, and Mr. and Mrs. Dorchester were down in her room. "Will you be comfortable up here?" George asked.

She grinned. "This used to be my room."

"Really?" He looked around the small room with interest.

"When my daddy was alive. He and Mama had the big front room and I slept right here." She patted the bed, which now had her crazy quilt spread over it. "After Daddy died, Mama and I moved our bedrooms downstairs. She said it was warmer down there in the wintertime. Then Mama started renting rooms up here. When Grandma came to live with us, she and Mama decided to share a room."

"Things changed a lot when your father died."

Lucy nodded.

"I'm sure you must miss him still."

She nodded again.

"Well . . ." He shoved his hands in his trouser pockets. "I'll leave you to it. I'm sure it must be just about time for dinner."

It wasn't until Lucy was seated at the table, where Mrs. Dorchester's chair was vacant, that she remembered she still hadn't told Mama about being late for the pageant practice and consequently losing her angel's wings. Lucy considered making this announcement now, but she couldn't quite think of the right way to say it.

"Who all wants to go to the Christmas pageant tonight?" George asked everyone at the table.

"Not Mrs. Dorchester, that's for sure." Mr. Dorchester shook his head. "Not me either."

"I want to go," Grandma said. "I'm sure Miriam does too." Mama just nodded as she reached for the salt shaker.

Lucy wanted to say she wasn't terribly eager to go but knew that would require a full explanation and wouldn't get her out of her responsibilities either.

"I'd like to go too," Veronica said. "I've been giving Lucy dramatic advice, and I'm most curious to see how well she performs."

Lucy felt her stomach twisting.

"I have an idea," George said. "Since my car holds only two passengers at the most, how about if I make two trips to town. I can drop Lucy and one other person earlier. Then I can take two others for the second trip." He pointed to Veronica. "Since you've been helping Lucy, maybe you'd like to be in the first trip."

Veronica looked uncertain. "Well . . . I suppose that would be all right. I could always walk around town a bit, just to kill time. It might be better than being stuck out here in the middle of nowhere."

It was settled, and Lucy knew there was no way out of it. She would've told Mama the whole story, but Mama was busy running back and forth for Mrs. Dorchester. Grandma had given her a bell to ring when she needed something, and it seemed the bell rang about every other minute.

"Time to go," George told Lucy and Veronica. "Are you ladies all ready?"

"Ready when you are." Veronica reached for her fur-trimmed coat.

Lucy grimaced. "Yes. I'll get my coat."

George wasn't even on the main road before Veronica began giving acting tips and advice to Lucy, telling her how to hold her chin high and to look directly out over the audience. Lucy exchanged glances with George, and it looked like he was suppressing laughter, although Lucy didn't see any humor in it.

"Remember what I said about thinking of yourself as an angel, Lucy. Think heavenly thoughts and put a sparkle in your eye and you'll be the—"

"*Stop!*" Lucy held up her hands. "Please, stop!"

"Well!" Veronica scowled at Lucy. "That's the thanks I get for all my help and advice. Humph!"

"I'm sorry," Lucy told her. "It's just that I don't get to play an angel after all."

"What?" Veronica looked surprised. "Why ever not?"

Looking down at her lap, Lucy explained that being late had cost her the role of angel. "I really wanted to be an angel this year."

"Well, that's too bad." Veronica made a tsk-tsk sound. "What are you playing then? A shepherd?"

"No . . . it's worse than that," Lucy admitted. "A sheep."

"A sheep?" Veronica made a snorting sort of laugh. "Are you kidding me?"

Lucy shook her head.

"What do you do? Say baa, baa?"

Lucy barely nodded.

Veronica laughed harder. "They are not going to believe this!"

"Who?" George asked.

"The people in Hollywood . . . I mean, when I get there. They are not going to believe I rode through a snowy night to see my little friend here playing the role of a farm animal." She threw back her head and laughed loudly.

Lucy felt that lump growing in her throat again. "I'm sorry," she said quietly.

"What?" Veronica turned to her. "I couldn't hear you over the engine, doll."

"I just said I'm sorry," Lucy repeated. "I can understand why you don't want to go now. Maybe you can ride back home with George or something."

"Hmm . . . not a bad idea."

George scowled at Veronica. "I'm looking forward to seeing Lucy as a sheep."

"I'm sure she will make a perfectly charming sheep," Veronica said lightly.

For the rest of the drive, the only sound was the motor rumbling and the crunching of snow beneath the tires. Lost in her thoughts, Lucy wondered how she would manage to find Mama and Grandma and explain everything . . . all before the pageant began.

"Here we are," George said as he pulled up in front of the church. As he helped her out of the car, he smiled. "Remember what I told you, Lucy. About the Lamb of God and his humble beginnings."

Lucy held up her chin and nodded. "I'll try to keep that in mind."

"Break a leg," Veronica called from the car.

Lucy frowned. "You mean like Mrs. Dorchester? But she only sprained—"

"No, silly." Veronica laughed. "It's a show biz saying. It's like good luck."

"Oh . . . thanks." Lucy waved to both of them, then hurried into the church. At least she wasn't late tonight. In fact, she was early. She slipped into the back of the sanctuary and into the last row, slumping down into the polished wooden pew and wishing she could think of a reason not to play a sheep tonight.

Before long, other children were coming in. Some were already in costume, and some went back to change. Lucy didn't need to worry about changing much since her costume was just the scratchy, smelly blanket. Even if she didn't grab it until the last minute, it would probably go unnoticed. Just like she would go unnoticed. Most of all, she wanted to keep a close watch on the door. She wanted to explain this business to Mama and Grandma.

Other parents and family members began filling the church pews, and Lucy was just getting worried that she wouldn't get a chance to speak to Mama when she and Grandma came in. "Oh, Mama," Lucy said as she jumped up from her seat.

"Lucy? What's the matter? Is something wrong?" Mama looked worried.

"Shouldn't you be in your costume?" Grandma asked.

"I have to tell you something first." Right in the aisle, with others looking on, Lucy spilled out the whole humiliating story of how she'd been late because of the movie. "Now I'm a sheep instead of an angel," she said breathlessly.

Grandma grinned. "Better a sheep than a goat."

"Why didn't you tell me this yesterday?" Mama asked.

"I wanted to, but—"

"Lucy Turnbull," Mrs. Babcock called from up front. "What are you doing down there? Come on, come on." She clapped her hands. "Front and center."

"I'm sorry, Mama," Lucy blurted. Then she turned and hurried up front.

All in all, it wasn't that bad playing a sheep again. Lucy put her heart into it as she thought hard about how a sheep might act. She bent down her head and pretended to eat grass, she said an authentic-sounding "baa" at appropriate times, and she even moved her body like she thought a sheep might do as she followed the shepherd up to the manger to see the baby Jesus, which was really Helen Krausner's old baby doll wrapped in a shredded sheet. Really, she thought, she was doing a much better job than the boys.

Even so, she was thankful when it was over. It was a relief to toss off her "costume" while other children struggled to peel off layers of cloaks and belts and headdresses. She hurried down to the church basement where the audience was to gather for holiday cookies and punch. She spotted George's tall head on the other side of the room, and as she made her way toward him, she spied Mama and Grandma too.

"Nicely done," George said as he patted her on the head.

"Thanks." She smiled. "I did my best."

He held up a frosted cookie shaped like a Christmas tree. "I saved this for you . . . in case you were interested. They were going fast."

"Thanks."

Mama gave Lucy an uncertain look but said nothing. Lucy supposed that Mama might be upset at her for keeping something from her. Still, Lucy wasn't sure what to do about it. Helen Krausner was coming her way. She motioned with her fingers for Lucy to come over and talk to her. Lucy wanted to turn and run the other way, but she went reluctantly.

"Where is your movie star friend?" Helen demanded. "You said she'd be here tonight."

"She decided not to come," Lucy told her.

Helen looked doubtful.

"She was disappointed when she found out I was only playing a sheep."

"Or else you just made her up."

"I didn't make her up," Lucy insisted. "She's real."

Helen rolled her eyes upward. "Says you."

"It's true. If you ask around town, I'm sure you'll hear that other people have seen her."

Helen shrugged. "I didn't think she'd really come. I could tell you were lying."

"I wasn't lying," Lucy protested. "Honest, Helen, Veronica is real."

Helen tilted her nose up, just the way Veronica sometimes did. "Well, I'll believe it when I see it." She turned and walked away.

"We'll have to pile into the car on the way home," George said as he led them outside. "It'll be cozy."

"Lucy can sit on my lap," Grandma offered.

Before long, they were all piled into the car with Mama in the middle and Lucy sitting on Grandma's bony knees. "Am I too heavy?" Lucy asked.

"No, dear, you're fine. Just lean back and relax." She wrapped her arms around Lucy's middle. "I'll pretend like you're my little Baby Lucy again."

Lucy giggled as she leaned back. "This is cozy," she said, "but I like it."

"How about if we sing Christmas carols," George suggested.

All the way home, they sang carols, laughing as one or the other stumbled over the words or the music. All in all, it was fun.

"That was almost like a sleigh ride," Lucy said as they got out.

"If it wasn't so late, I'd make us all some hot chocolate," Grandma said.

"I'm full of cookies and punch," George assured her.

"And I'm tired," Mama said. "Mrs. Dorchester is a demanding patient, and I suspect tomorrow won't be much easier."

"Too bad she can't stay with her niece while she's recovering," George said as they went inside.

"Hopefully she'll heal quickly," Mama whispered.

Inside the house, everyone said quiet good-nights, going their separate ways. To Lucy's surprise, Mama didn't even come up to her new room to help her get ready for bed or listen to her prayers. Perhaps she really was tired. Or maybe Grandma had told her what Lucy had said—that she was too old for bedtime help. Maybe Lucy was. Or perhaps Mama was embarrassed that Lucy hadn't played an angel tonight. Especially since the pageant program had mistakenly listed Lucy as an angel. More likely, Mama was just disappointed that Lucy hadn't told her the whole truth sooner.

Whatever it was, Lucy felt too tired to figure it out. Besides, it was well past her bedtime, and today had been a busy one. If Mama was up here, she would probably tell Lucy to go to bed! She climbed under the covers and made an attempt at her usual prayer, but before long, she felt herself drifting.

Lucy woke to the sound of voices just outside her door. Sitting up in bed, it took her a moment to remember where she was—in her old upstairs room. She saw a slit of light under her door and could tell it was George and Veronica who were talking in the hallway. Curious as to why they were still up and conversing, she tiptoed out of bed and put her ear to the door.

"I want out of here, George," Veronica was saying in an emotional voice. "I swear I cannot abide another day out here—in the middle of nowhere."

"Then you should leave," he calmly told her.

"How?" she demanded.

"Keep your voice down," he warned.

"Fine, but how can I possibly leave unless you go with me?" she hissed at him.

"Take a train," he suggested in a firm but quiet tone. "Like I've told you to do dozens of times already. Trains pass through every—"

"I know, I know. You keep saying that, George. But I—I just can't." She made a sniffing sound, like she was crying.

"Of course you can." His voice grew more gentle. "Lots of trains pass through Flagstaff on their way to Los Angeles, and I can—"

"Don't you understand?" Her voice turned small and sweet, like a little girl. "I can't take a train, George. I just can't. Why don't you understand that?"

Lucy pressed her ear closer to the door, causing a board to creak. George cleared his throat, and Lucy heard the sound of shuffling feet. "Maybe we should go down to the front room to talk about this," he whispered. "We might be disturbing Lucy."

Just like that, they were gone. Lucy stood there a bit longer, straining her ears to hear, but all she could pick up was a muffled conversation, and only just barely. Tempted to tiptoe down the stairs to hear the rest of their conversation, she remembered how several of the steps had loud squeaks and would probably reveal her spying ways, which might prove embarrassing. Still extremely curious, she went back to bed and wondered what was going on down there.

12

Lucy felt excited when she woke up the next morning. Today was Christmas Eve! Just the same, she knew there were chores to do and the chickens needed tending. Even though it was before dawn, she crawled out of bed, dressing quietly since she remembered she was upstairs with the guests now, then tiptoed down the stairs, where the third step from the top loudly creaked, and hurried to put on her outer clothes. Grandma wasn't in the kitchen yet, but there were still some red coals in the woodstove, which meant Mama or Grandma had fed it in the middle of the night. Lucy paused to load some more wood into it, then headed outside.

As she carried the chicken bucket across the yard, she was surprised to see that fresh snow had fallen during the night. A half moon, still hanging on the western horizon, was illuminating everything in a magical way. As she trudged through the crunchy snow, where no footprints showed and no shoveling had been done, she realized that she was the first one up this morning. For some reason that filled her with a feeling of high anticipation. Christmas Eve morning, and Lucy was the first one up to enjoy it!

She broke the ice and filled the water and food troughs. The chickens were still sleeping on their roosts in the henhouse, and she knew that during winter they could be deep sleepers. In fact, she'd heard some chickens could sleep so soundly that a fox could slip in and snatch them unawares. Thanks to the sturdy fence around the chicken yard, that had not happened. She crept quietly over to the nesting boxes, peeking inside just like she always did, and to her delight discovered seven eggs. Since she'd forgotten to bring the egg basket, she carefully slipped some of the eggs into her coat pockets, carrying the rest of them in her hands.

As she walked toward the house, she noticed that the eastern sky was turning pink, casting a rosy light over the snow. It was so beautiful that Lucy had to just stand there and look. Then she saw that the lights were on in the kitchen, and realizing she was hungry, she hurried inside to find Grandma, still wearing her housecoat, putting a pot of water on the stove.

"Eggs!" Lucy exclaimed as she burst into the warm, bright room.

"Oh, my!" Grandma examined the three eggs in Lucy's hands. "George's light trick worked. And just in time because I wanted to do some baking today and the recipe calls for three."

"There are more." Lucy handed over the precious treasure. *"Seven!"*

"Not enough to serve all the guests." Grandma set the eggs

in a blue bowl. "But I don't see any reason why you couldn't have one, Lucy, if you'd like."

"*Yes!*" Lucy smacked her lips as she peeled off her coat and mittens.

"Your mama is tending to Mrs. Dorchester," Grandma said as she cracked the egg and dropped it onto a cast iron skillet.

"Poor Mama."

"I've a mind to call up the Farleys and tell them to come get their relatives." She sighed. "Except that we need the money."

Lucy nodded. "I know. I can help with Mrs. Dorchester too," she offered as she washed her hands at the sink.

"We should charge the Dorchesters for nursing care too," Grandma said a bit tersely.

"The sunrise is so beautiful this morning." Lucy gazed out the window as she sat at the kitchen table. "Look, Grandma, all the snow is turning pinkish red now."

Grandma came over to peer outside, then shook her head in a dismal way. "You know what they say about a red sunrise."

"What?"

"Red sky at morning, sailors take warning; red sky at night, sailors delight."

"What does that mean?"

"It means if there's a red sunrise, the weather will be bad. But if there's a red sunset, the weather will be good."

"But there aren't sailors in Arizona," Lucy pointed out.

Grandma laughed. "That's true enough."

Mama greeted them as she came into the kitchen. "Is that an egg I smell, or am I dreaming?" She peered at the stove.

"Lucy found seven eggs," Grandma proclaimed. "So I figured it wouldn't hurt to reward her with one. However, we won't have enough for the guests."

"Hopefully they won't smell it cooking."

"Oh, dear." Grandma slid the sunny-side up egg onto a plate and set it in front of Lucy. "You'd better hurry and eat that."

"Maybe we could spare an egg or two for Mrs. Dorchester," Mama said. "Since she eats in her room. It might improve her spirits."

"I'm sure they can use some improving too." Grandma patted Mama on the back. "I don't envy you, although Lucy has offered to help with her."

Mama bent down to kiss Lucy on the top of the head. "You're a dear, Lucy, but I think we should leave Mrs. Dorchester to me. In some ways I feel sorry for her. She would really rather be at home with her injury. I can't blame her."

"I wish she were at home too," Grandma added.

Lucy beamed at Mama. Maybe she wasn't angry at Lucy after all.

"I realized after I went to bed that I completely forgot to tuck you in and hear your prayers," Mama said contritely. "I'm sorry, dear."

"It's all right, Mama." Lucy smiled. "I know you were tired and I was—" She was interrupted by the tinkling of a bell.

"Oh, dear." Mama sighed. "Time to fetch the bedpan."

"What's a bedpan?" Lucy asked as Mama left.

Grandma chuckled. "Don't ask."

Lucy shrugged and returned to eating her delightful egg. No

140

matter what Grandma said about red skies and sailors, Lucy felt certain that this was going to be a good day.

She had just finished up the egg and was setting the breakfast table when Mama returned, passing through the dining room with a perplexed expression. "I cannot believe it!" she exclaimed as she went into the kitchen.

"Believe what?" Grandma asked.

"What they have done," Mama said in a hushed tone.

Lucy paused now, holding a plate in her hand, straining to try to hear each word.

"They have left."

"Who has left?" Grandma demanded.

"Veronica and George."

"*What?*"

"On my way from the bathroom upstairs, after taking care of the bedpan, I noticed the front bedroom door was open and the sunrise was streaming in the big window, and I happened to glance inside the room."

"*And?*"

"And the room had been vacated. The bed was unmade, so it appears it was slept in, but all of her luggage—everything—was gone, Mother. The closet was bare."

"George too? You're sure he's gone?"

"His door was closed, but I knocked quietly, and when he didn't answer, I peeked in his room to see the bed was neatly made as usual, but it looked as if he'd cleared out as well. Then I came downstairs and looked out the front room window to discover that his car is gone too."

"What does this mean?"

"It means that they sneaked out in the middle of the night, Mother." Mama let out a low groan. "And they stiffed us on the bill."

"Oh, my! I simply cannot believe it, Miriam. George did not seem like the type to do something—"

"Well, he did, Mother. We might as well get over it."

"Oh, Miriam."

"Don't waste your pity on me, Mother. I'm going out to the barn now."

Lucy was still frozen in place, the plate in her hand. How could this be true? George wouldn't do something like this! She set down the plate and dashed upstairs, peeking into the rooms to see it was just as Mama had described. She looked out the window, and sure enough, George's car was gone. How could this happen?

As Lucy went downstairs, she remembered the conversation she'd overheard last night and how Veronica had sounded so unhappy and wanted to leave. Maybe George had driven her to the train station this morning! With this hope in mind, she hurried to finish setting the table, then grabbed her coat and dashed out to the barn. "Mama," she cried as she went inside to find Mama fueling the woodstove. "I think I know where George is!"

"What?" Mama turned to look at Lucy.

"I think I know what happened, Mama." She noticed that Mama had tears on her cheeks. She'd only seen Mama cry a few times, and it always felt horrible. Feeling a lump in her own throat, Lucy went over and put her arms around Mama's waist,

looking up and explaining about the conversation she'd overheard last night. "Maybe George took Veronica to Flagstaff,"
she said eagerly, "to get on a train."

Mama knelt down now, looking directly into Lucy's eyes. "I
had thought the same thing, Lucy. But I looked outside to see
there weren't any car tracks in the fresh snow."

"But maybe the snow fell this morning," Lucy suggested.

"I got up around two in the morning to get a bit of milk
and to load up more wood on the fire," Mama told her. "It was
already snowing then."

"Oh . . ." Lucy tried to grasp what this meant.

"They must have left shortly after you heard them talking,
Lucy. Maybe around midnight." Mama sighed. "That was about
eight hours ago. Even in the snow, it would take only an hour
or so to reach Flagstaff."

Lucy felt tears filling her eyes now. Was it true that George
really was gone? Gone for good?

"We'd better go back inside and help Grandma with breakfast." Mama stood, using the bottom of her apron to wipe her
eyes. "How many places did you set on the table?"

"Oh, that's right." Lucy nodded. "I'll run back and remove
two."

Mama nodded sadly. "Tell Grandma I'll be in shortly."

Lucy felt like her feet were weighted down with lead as she
trudged back through the snow to the house. Maybe Grandma
was right. Maybe red sky in the morning really was a bad sign
after all.

Breakfast was a somber affair. Fortunately, the usually quiet

Mr. Dorchester didn't inquire about the missing guests, so no explanations were needed. He seemed to have plenty on his mind as he shoveled in his oatmeal. Perhaps he was worried about his wife. Lucy just hoped he wasn't planning a way for them to leave too. Because right now they needed the room and board money more than ever.

As Lucy helped with the breakfast dishes, she decided that she would do whatever she could to make Mrs. Dorchester as comfortable and happy as possible. Not only would it lighten Mama's load, but it might encourage the Dorchesters to remain here. However, it didn't take long before Lucy agreed with Grandma that perhaps it would be best if Mrs. Dorchester went to stay with her relatives nearby. Of course, she kept her thoughts to herself. Today was not a day for complaining. Grandma was in a foul mood, and Mama was keeping herself busier than ever.

"This tea is cold," Mrs. Dorchester told Lucy in midafternoon.

Lucy touched the outside of the teacup to feel that it was quite warm. "It feels hot to me."

"You are a child. Naturally, it would feel hot to you." She tipped the cup to her thin, pale lips to try it again and then made a face that looked as if she'd been stabbed with a pin. "But it is most definitely cold! Please tell your grandmother to make me a fresh cup." Before Lucy could take the tray away, Mrs. Dorchester snatched up the three ginger cookies.

As Lucy set the tea tray in the kitchen, she moaned. "Mrs. Dorchester said the tea is cold and to make another cup."

"Apparently she liked the cookies." Grandma slid the tea kettle to a hotter spot on the stove.

"How's Mama doing?"

"She's shoveling snow . . . again."

"Oh . . ."

Grandma peered curiously at Lucy now. "Why do you ask?"

"I know all about it, Grandma," Lucy confessed. "I know Mama's sad because George left . . . and all that." She didn't really want to go into it, to hear the awful story rehashed again. She just wanted to know that Mama was going to be all right.

Grandma tossed a dirty spoon into the sink and shook her head. "It's just a shame . . . a doggone shame! He seemed like such a nice fellow too. And to do that . . . and at Christmas! Well, I can hardly speak of it."

Lucy felt the lump returning to her own throat now. "I know."

"All I can say is good riddance." Grandma frowned as she reached for the flour canister, dipping in her measuring cup. *"Good riddance."*

Lucy went to look out the window. The sky was getting darker, heavy and gray. "Do you think it's going to snow again?" she asked quietly.

"Probably."

Lucy looked over to where George's car used to be parked, to where he had snuck away in the middle of the night. Suddenly she remembered something. "The old car!" she cried as she ran to the door, grabbing her coat.

"What?" Grandma called.

"I'll be right back." Lucy ran outside and through the snow and around the barn, back to the lean-to garage her daddy had built when she was little. There was their old car, all cleaned up and looking surprisingly nice. She got inside of it and wondered if the engine worked. Of course, she had no way of knowing. But it sure looked promising, cleaned up the way it was. She considered telling Mama about it but then realized that it would only get her hopes up . . . and what if it didn't run? Maybe it was best to wait a while. Still, it was nice to see.

"What was that all about?" Grandma asked when Lucy returned to the kitchen.

"Oh . . . nothing."

Grandma filled a teapot with steaming water, put the lid on, then slipped a crocheted tea cozy around it. "Well, here's a whole pot of very hot tea," Grandma told her. "Get it directly to Mrs. Dorchester. She's been ringing that bell almost nonstop for the last few minutes, and my nerves are wearing thin."

Lucy glanced at the loaf of pumpkin bread fresh out of the oven. "Should you send her a slice of that too?"

Grandma frowned, then nodded. "You're probably right, Lucy. It might help to keep her quiet for a spell. At least long enough for me to get dinner ready."

"Do you think we can still string popcorn tonight?" Lucy asked a bit timidly.

Grandma's face softened as she set two slices of pumpkin bread on a saucer. "Of course we can, Lucy. We'll have hot cocoa too." She patted Lucy's head. "You'll have to forgive me for being out of sorts."

"I do, Grandma." Lucy picked up the tray. "I understand."

"Yes," Grandma said sadly. "I'll bet you do, dear."

After dinner, Mr. Dorchester turned in early, so only Mama

and Grandma and Lucy remained in the front room with the oversized and sparsely decorated Christmas tree. True to her word, Grandma made hot cocoa, and they sat around listening to the Christmas songs on the radio and stringing popcorn. Lucy thought that in spite of all that had gone on today, they were having a pretty good time.

But sometimes, as she was reaching for more fluffy white pieces of popcorn to slip onto her sharp needle, Lucy would glance at Mama. If Mama didn't know Lucy was looking, the sadness would show in her eyes. Lucy didn't know if Mama would ever smile again, and it cut Lucy to the core. Plus, she couldn't help feeling somewhat responsible for this pain. After all, hadn't she encouraged Mama to put her hopes in George? Talking him up and telling Mama how she thought he was falling in love. Had Lucy imagined these things? Now she blamed herself for Mama's broken heart. Because that's what Lucy thought it was—a broken heart.

Lucy wished she'd never seen George and Veronica in town that day, never invited them to stay at the house, never welcomed them into her life . . . and never trusted them with her secrets. Maybe this was what Mama was talking about when she said that Lucy would see things differently when she was a grown-up. Maybe Lucy was closer to being a grown-up than she realized. However, she would follow Mama and Grandma's example. Lucy would keep up a brave front. After all, it was Christmas Eve.

13

Although Mama had told Lucy she could stay up past her bedtime tonight, Lucy wasn't so sure she wanted to. After she'd finished her last garland of popcorn, one that was taller than she was, she admitted that she was tired and happy to go to bed at her usual time.

"I'm with you, Lucy." Grandma stood and stretched her back. "It's been a long day, and I'm plumb worn out."

"Goodnight, Grandma." Lucy went over and kissed her cheek. "Goodnight, Mama." Lucy was ready to give her a kiss too, but Mama stood.

"Do you mind if I help you get ready for bed tonight?" she asked Lucy hopefully. "Or are you really too big?"

Lucy smiled. "I was hoping you'd ask."

Just like old times, Mama helped Lucy out of her clothes and into her nightgown. She brushed and rebraided Lucy's hair and listened to her prayers. But she didn't turn the light off right away. Instead she reached over for Lucy's hand, giving it a warm squeeze in her own.

"I know something is wrong," she told Lucy. "I can see it in your eyes."

Lucy swallowed hard, looking away.

"I suspect it has to do with George," Mama said quietly, "and the way he left so suddenly."

Lucy just nodded.

"I know George was a very good friend to you while he was here, and I suspect it's been hard on you and that you're feeling sad and—"

"I'm not sad for me," Lucy said suddenly. "Not really." She considered this. More than anything she wanted to be completely honest with Mama. "Oh, I guess I'm a little sad for me. Maybe even a lot. But most of all I'm sad for you, Mama."

"Oh . . ." Mama just nodded. "Well, you probably have figured out that I'm a little sad too."

"I feel like it's all my fault." Lucy started to cry now. "I did everything all wrong. I invited George and Veronica into our house. I trusted them. I thought they would pay for their rooms and they didn't. And I made you believe George loved you and—"

"Wait a minute, Lucy." Mama pointed a forefinger in the air. "You did *not* make me believe anything. If I believed something, it's because I chose to believe it."

"But I saw how he looked at you. I told you things that—"

"I'm a grown woman, Lucy. I have eyes to see with."

With tears pouring down her cheeks, Lucy sat up and wrapped her arms around Mama's neck. "I'm just so sorry, Mama. I wish

I could go back and change everything back to how it used to be. If I found a genie in a lamp, I'd make a wish that George and Veronica never came to visit us. That I'd never seen them in town that day."

Mama stroked Lucy's hair. "But maybe it was a good thing they came."

Lucy leaned back to look into Mama's face. How could she possibly think that? George and Veronica had brought nothing but pain—and they didn't even pay their bill.

"Maybe it showed me something . . ." Mama sighed. "Something about myself . . . something I needed to be reminded of."

"What?"

Mama made a smile—or maybe it was just half a smile, but it seemed genuine to Lucy. "Maybe it showed me that it might be possible to fall in love again, Lucy. Someday . . ."

Lucy blinked. "Really, Mama?"

Mama nodded. "Maybe so."

"But does it hurt to feel like that?"

Mama shrugged. "Some kinds of hurts can be good for us." She helped Lucy lean back into her pillow, tucking the covers snugly back around her chin again. "Remember that time you got a bad splinter in your thumb and how much it hurt to pull it out? But when it was done, you knew it was a good hurt because the sliver was gone and the wound would get better. So it was a healing kind of hurt. Does that make any sense?"

Lucy nodded, although she wasn't sure she really understood. Mostly she was just relieved to see that Mama wasn't as sad as Lucy had imagined.

"Don't feel bad for my sake. And please, do not blame your-self." Mama leaned over and kissed Lucy's forehead again. "Be-cause, really, I am fine."

"I'm fine too, Mama."

"Don't forget, tomorrow is Christmas day. I'm sure we'll all have a very good day now, won't we?"

"Yes." Lucy smiled as she remembered the presents she'd made and wrapped. "Yes, we most certainly will!"

Mama stood and pulled the string on the light. "Good night, darling."

"Good night, Mama."

Lucy closed her eyes and let out a long sigh of relief. Oh, she still felt a little bit sad and sore inside . . . kind of like her thumb had felt before it got well again. But she did feel hope-ful. Mama was going to be all right. And she'd almost smiled again tonight.

Lucy was just starting to drift off to sleep when she heard the sound of clumping and thumping and then footsteps in the house. She sat up in bed and listened hard—if Tommy Farley hadn't ruined her childish hopes of Santa Claus visiting on Christmas Eve, she might have actually thought that he'd come to her house after all. As it was, she wanted to find out what was going on. Silently slipping out of bed, she tiptoed to the head of the stairs and, clinging to the stair rail post, she listened.

"George?" Mama's voice sounded shrill with surprise. "What on earth are you doing here?"

"I thought I was staying here," he told her. "But I'm terribly sorry to get in so late. I was hoping everyone would still be up . . . since it's Christmas Eve."

Unable to believe her ears, Lucy ran down the stairs and into the front room, nearly crashing into Mama. *"George!"* Lucy exclaimed. "You came back!"

He gave her a sheepish grin as he removed his snow-coated hat. "I hadn't meant to be so late and to wake up the entire house. But yes, like a bad penny, I'm back."

"Where on earth have you been?" Mama asked. "And where is Veronica?"

"It's a long story." George started to peel off his coat, taking it over to the hall tree by the door to hang it up.

Mama frowned at Lucy. "You were in bed, young lady."

"But you told me I could stay up past my bedtime tonight," Lucy reminded her.

Mama nodded. "I suppose you deserve to hear this too." She reached for the crocheted afghan blanket on the back of the sofa. "Wrap up in this if you plan to stay and listen."

Lucy draped herself in the blanket, and soon they were all seated as George explained what had happened. "Veronica decided that she had to leave here," he began. "Unfortunately she made this decision shortly after midnight. It seemed a little crazy, but I was so relieved that she wanted to go that I finally decided to accommodate her. So I drove her to the railway station in Flagstaff."

"In the middle of the night?" Mama seemed a little doubtful.

"And you took your things," Lucy added.

He looked confused. "My things?"

"Your room was cleared out, George." Mama frowned at him.

He gave her a bewildered smile. "Did you check the closet and the drawers?"

"Well, no . . . but all of Veronica's things were gone . . . and your room looked vacated, and—"

"I just like to put my things away," he told her. "If you'd looked a bit more, you would've seen that everything, including my suitcase, was still here."

"Oh . . ." Mama's brow creased. "So you took Veronica to the Flagstaff train station . . . and then?"

"As you know, it was late at night. As it turned out, the next westbound train didn't leave until six in the morning. So I gave Veronica enough money for a ticket and a room for the night, and then I dropped her off at a nearby hotel."

"She really was penniless?" Lucy asked.

"That's what she told me," he said. "Just last night, in fact. Before that I had no idea she was broke."

"That's what she said to me too," Lucy confessed. "But she had enough to take us to the movies."

"Veronica Grant had *no* money?" Mama looked somewhat suspicious now. "Even though she dressed so finely, had so many expensive things?"

Lucy explained about Veronica's movie friend who'd taken all her money and dropped her off on the side of the road. "That's when George gave her a ride."

"Then how did she plan to pay for her room here?" Mama asked.

George held up his hands. "I have no idea. But don't worry. I plan to cover that for her too."

"But why *should* you?" Mama demanded. "Furthermore, why are you buying Veronica Grant train tickets and hotel rooms and paying her room and board, George? What do you owe her?"

"I don't owe her a thing." George held his hands palms upward, with a puzzled and somewhat tired look. "I suppose it was to get her out of your hair and on her way, Miriam."

"I heard Veronica talking last night," Lucy told Mama. "She sounded really eager to get out of here. She'd told me lots of times before that she wanted to leave and go to Hollywood. But she had no money." Lucy glanced at George. "I think she had another reason for staying too."

"What was that?" George asked.

"I think she wanted George to marry her." Lucy directed this to Mama.

"What?" Mama's brows lifted.

George laughed. "Well, trust me, there was never the slightest chance of that happening, Miriam. Not a snowball's chance in Tahiti."

"Why not?" Mama folded her arms across her front with her head tilted to one side.

His eyes twinkled. "Because Veronica is *not* the kind of woman that interests me."

"Even though she is so beautiful?" Lucy asked him.

He looked directly at Lucy now. "I'll be honest with you. When I first saw Veronica standing alongside the road, she did turn my head somewhat. For a moment I actually thought I was seeing things. But after she got in the car and as I got to know her—and, believe me, that didn't take more than a few hours—I knew without a shadow of doubt that Veronica Grant, as pretty as she might be, would never be the one for me. But by then I couldn't manage to shake her off. I tried to drop her off a number of times, but she kept making excuses to travel with me. I had no idea she was broke." He rubbed his chin. "Come to think of it, that explains a lot."

Mama stood now, pacing back and forth across the room as if she was trying to grasp all this, as was Lucy. Then Mama went over to look out the big front window. "I didn't hear your car drive up, George. Where is it?"

"That's part of the reason I'm so late."

"What happened to your car?" Lucy asked with concern.

"It broke down again." He chuckled. "I'm starting to think that it's not just lemon yellow but a lemon as well."

"Huh?" Lucy had no idea what he meant.

"How did your car break down?" Mama asked. "And where is it?"

"It happened last night. I was on my way back here, hoping that I'd slip back into the house and into bed and no one would be the wiser. Then I'd be the hero at the breakfast table when I announced to everyone that Veronica was on a train to Los Angeles. It seemed a good plan to me."

"That would've been nice," Lucy told him.

"Instead, I was stuck in a broken down car, just outside of Flagstaff, and just as the snow was starting to fall. It was coming down heavy and I wasn't sure if I was going to be buried alive in a snowdrift. But I pulled out the car robe and wrapped myself up in it and said my prayers and fell asleep. Well, I slept off and on. I did a lot of praying and thinking too."

"Weren't you scared?" Lucy asked.

"To be honest, I was. But I also had a sense of peace too. Somehow I knew everything would work out. Finally, about an hour after sunrise, which was one of the most beautiful sights I've ever seen, a farm truck happened along, and the good man gave me a ride back into Flagstaff."

George explained how he had to wait several hours in a Flagstaff coffee shop for a tow truck. "Being that it was Christmas Eve, not everyone was eager to work." Then he told how his car was towed to Hempley's Garage, but due to a couple of slippery incidents, it took nearly three hours.

"Why didn't you just go to a Flagstaff garage?" Mama asked.

"Because I was staying here," George told her. "And Hempley's is nearby. I tried to call the house this afternoon, but no one answered."

"It's been a very busy day," Mama told him. "We had Christmas songs on the radio, and we might not have heard the phone ringing."

"Well, anyway, I had dinner at the café, and after Hempley finally had a chance to look under the hood, he told me that it was only a broken belt. He offered to fix it, but I felt bad for taking him away from his family. I told him it could wait until after Christmas, and then I walked on out here." He shook his head. "Thanks to the snow, I somehow wandered down the wrong driveway, so it took even longer than expected." He sighed. "It's been a very long day."

"At least you're back." Lucy threw off the afghan now and ran over to hug him. "I'm so glad you didn't stiff us on the bill, George."

"*Lucy!*" Mama looked aghast, but George just laughed.

Lucy grimaced. "That's what Grandma said."

"Well, I don't want to hear you repeating everything your grandmother says."

"Sorry." Lucy turned back to George. "Still, I'm so glad you're back."

"Perhaps you should go to bed now," Mama suggested.

George nodded. "Especially if you expect Santa Claus to show up."

Lucy gave him a tolerant smile. "That's all right. I'm old enough to know that Santa Claus isn't real."

He looked surprised. "What makes you so certain?"

"Tommy Farley told me."

"And Tommy Farley is an expert on such things?" George asked. "Has he been to the North Pole and done investigations?"

"No. He's only ten."

"Ten years old and you listened to him?"

Lucy felt a bit foolish now. Come to think of it, Tommy wasn't right about a lot of things.

"If I were you, I would get myself to bed and to sleep as quickly as possible." George went over to look out the window. "Just in case Santa is passing over your house right now and deciding not to—"

"I'm going!" She made a beeline for the stairs. "Good night, Mama. Good night, George." Faster than lightning, she zipped up the stairs, leaped into bed, closed her eyes, and tried her best to go to sleep. But first she told God thank you for bringing George back to them. She didn't know how long George would stay or if he loved Mama, but at least he hadn't run out on them like they'd thought.

14

Once again, Lucy woke up before the sun. But since it was Christmas morning, she couldn't stay in bed a minute longer. She still had her doubts about Santa Claus visiting last night, but she was so glad George was back that she didn't even care. She dressed as quietly as she could and tiptoed out to see that George's door was still closed. She hoped he was sleeping in since he must have been tired after his long day yesterday.

When she got downstairs, it appeared as if no one else was up down here either. She silently gathered the chicken bucket and egg basket and went outside. By the light of the moon, which was nearly down to the western horizon, she made her way out to the chickens. Just like yesterday, her footprints were the first tracks in last night's snow. She tended to the chickens, tossing out some extra grain since today was Christmas. Before she left, she checked the nests and was delighted to find nine eggs! Carefully loading them into the wire basket, she could see the sky lightening in the east and knew it wouldn't be long until the sun was up.

With lighthearted steps, she was just heading back to the house when she noticed what looked like smoke coming from the back porch. Alarmed that something was on fire, she nearly dropped the egg basket and bucket, but then George stepped out and waved his pipe at her. "Merry Christmas," he called out in a quiet voice.

"Oh!" She let out a relieved sigh as she went onto the porch. "Merry Christmas, George. My goodness, when I saw the smoke, I thought the house was on fire."

He frowned at his pipe. "Oh, maybe I shouldn't be—"

"No, no," she told him. "It's all right. It just surprised me." She held up her egg basket. "The hens are laying eggs again!"

His eyes lit up. "The light trick worked!"

"Seven eggs yesterday and nine today. That's sixteen total!"

"Your math is good, Lucy." He grinned. "Now, how about if you put the eggs in the house and then come help me with something?"

"Sure." She opened the door, and seeing that the kitchen was still semidark, she quietly set the eggs on the table, then returned to see what George wanted.

"Come with me," he said as he led her toward the barn and then around behind it. "I have something to show you."

"I think I know what it is," she confessed. "I saw the car yesterday, George. I couldn't believe how good it looks. But does it run?"

He grinned. "You'll see."

Sure enough, the car did start and it did run. George even took her for a little ride. "Just to get the engine warmed up," he told her. "Then we'll surprise your mother."

"She'll be so happy." Lucy looked out the window as the sun crested the horizon. Today it was golden and bright . . . almost like a promise that things were going to get better.

"This is a good old car," George told her as he turned around to head back for home.

"It sure is." Lucy beamed at him.

"I think it's a better car than my roadster."

Lucy was surprised. "But your car is so fancy and nice, George. I'm surprised you'd say that."

He shrugged. "Fancy and nice doesn't always get you where you want to go, Lucy."

She remembered him telling about being stuck on the side of the road and nodded. "I guess not."

"Anyway, I told Mr. Hempley that I might be interested in selling my roadster to him."

"You'd sell your car?" She turned to stare at him. "How would you get to California?"

He made what looked like a nervous smile. "Maybe I won't go . . ."

"Won't go?" She tried to grasp what this meant. "Do you mean you'd stay here with us in Maple Grove?"

"If your mother would let me."

Lucy didn't know what to say.

"What do you think? Would your mother be interested in a

new husband? For that matter, Lucy, would you be interested in a new daddy?"

Lucy swallowed hard. This seemed too good to be true.

"Maybe I'm rushing things," he said now.

"No," Lucy said quickly. "No . . . I was just thinking, George. I do think Mama would be interested in a new husband. I know I'm interested in a new daddy." She turned and smiled at him. "As long as it's the right one . . . someone just like you!"

He grinned and drove the car a little faster. Soon they were parked in front of the house. "Why don't you go see if your mother is up yet and if she wants to come out and—" But Lucy was already jumping out of the car and running into the house.

"Mama, Mama," she cried out as she went inside.

"Lucy!" Grandma looked alarmed. "What's wrong?"

"Nothing's wrong," Lucy exclaimed. "Where's Mama?"

"She just went out to the barn. But what's this excitement? I heard George is back, but what are you carrying on—"

"I'll explain it all later," Lucy said breathlessly. "First I need to find Mama." She ran for the back door. "Merry Christmas, Grandma," she called over her shoulder as she shot out. She spotted Mama coming out of the barn now. "Mama," she cried out, pointing to the car in front of the house. "Look!"

Mama's face was full of wonder. "Who is that and what's going on?"

Lucy grabbed Mama's hand. "Come and see."

"Merry Christmas," George said as he hopped out of the car.

"Is that our old car?" Mama asked with wide eyes.

164

"And it runs, Mama!" Lucy pulled her over to the passenger side. "Get in! George will take you for a ride."

"Just a minute." Mama held up her hands with a troubled look. "I have some questions first."

"What's wrong?" Lucy felt worried now. "I told George it was all right to work on the car. I didn't think you'd mind. You're not mad, are you?"

Mama shook her head with a perplexed expression. "No, I think it's just fine—it's wonderful—that George fixed our car." She looked at him with glistening eyes. "Thank you very much, George."

"Then what is it?" Lucy demanded

Mama pointed back to the barn. "Have you been in the barn this morning, Lucy?"

"No, but I did feed the chickens. Do you want me to bring in some wood and—"

"That's not what I meant, Lucy." Mama glanced at George. "I just wondered if you'd gone into the barn at all."

"No, Mama." Lucy was confused now.

"Maybe you should."

Lucy nodded. "All right. I can do that. But will you go for a ride with George now? He really wants to show you how the car is working so nicely, don't you, George?"

He grinned. "I most certainly do." He made a slight bow in front of Mama. "It would be my pleasure. That is, if you would care to join me, Miriam."

Mama looked from George to Lucy, then smiled. "I would love to take a ride with you, George."

Lucy felt a wave of relief rushing through her. "Good. I'll go to the barn," she promised. She watched as George helped Mama into the car, then got in and drove slowly down the driveway toward the road.

Confused as to why Mama wanted her to go to the barn, Lucy trudged across the yard again and slid open the big door. Mama had already started a fire in the stove, but it didn't look as if she was doing any laundry this morning. Why should she do laundry on Christmas morning? Lucy was about to leave when she heard a shuffling sound. She jumped. What was that? Had a wild animal gotten trapped in here somehow? Carefully backing toward the door and getting ready to make a run for the house, she heard another sound . . . like a nickering, followed by more shuffling and then a clunk.

"*What?*" Lucy stopped backing up and instead walked slowly toward the box stalls in the rear of the barn. As her eyes adjusted to the dim light, she couldn't believe what she was seeing. In fact, it took her breath away. "*Smoky!*" she cried as she ran to get a better look at the pony. "What are you doing here?"

He moved his head up and down and let out a little neighing sound as if he was glad to see her, and she let herself into the stall and began to stroke his mane.

"Oh, Smoky," she said gently. "How on earth did you get here?" She pressed her face into his neck, smelling his horsey smell and feeling his soft, fuzzy coat against her cheek. Tears of joy filled her eyes. "This really is the best Christmas ever," she whispered to him. "The best Christmas in the whole wide world." Lucy wrapped her arms around his neck and closed her eyes, whispering a prayer of thanks to God. He had answered every single one of her Christmas prayers—and then some!

Now she noticed a bridle hanging on a peg. Over one of the stall walls was a small, nicely worn saddle and blanket. "Come on, Smoky," she said as she slipped his bridle onto his muzzle. "We should take a little walk." She thought she remembered how to do this from spending time at Clara's farm and working with their old, slow plow horses, back before the Saunders family moved away, but it took a few minutes to get it in place and secured.

Feeling happy and proud, she now led Smoky out of the barn and over to the house. "I'm going to get you a treat," she told him as she walked him up to the porch and tethered him there. "You be a good boy and wait."

She ran into the house and making a frantic attempt to pour out her jumbled story to Grandma, she grabbed an apple from the cooler and was heading back out the door.

"What on earth?" Grandma stopped her, putting her hand on Lucy's forehead as if she thought she had a fever.

"Come and see for yourself," Lucy called as she dashed back outside to make certain she wasn't imagining the whole thing. But Smoky was still there, patiently waiting by the porch.

"*My word!*" Grandma exclaimed as she came over to peer at the pony.

"Here you go, Smoky." Lucy held the apple out in her open palm, grinning at her bewildered grandmother. *"See!"*

"What in the world?" Grandma ran her hand down Smoky's fuzzy back. "Where did *that* come from?"

"He was in the barn, Grandma!"

"But how in tarnation did he get there?"

"I'm not sure." Lucy considered this. "There weren't any tracks in the snow this morning. I know because I was the first one up." She laughed as she stroked Smoky's mane. "Maybe Santa Claus brought him."

Grandma shook her head. "Well, I'll be. I'll be." She came around to get a better look at Smoky's face. "I know you're over the moon about this, Lucy. But what will your mother say?"

Lucy pointed to where the old Model T was rumbling toward them. "I'm sure you'll find out soon enough."

"What?" Grandma pulled her cardigan around her more tightly as she leaned forward to squint at the road. "Who is that?"

Lucy quickly explained how George had fixed their old car. "It was our secret," she divulged. "Now George says he might sell his roadster to Mr. Hempley."

"Whatever for?" Grandma put her hand to her cheek as if she was completely befuddled.

Lucy giggled. "Maybe George thinks one car is enough for one family."

Grandma's eyes got very wide now.

Lucy continued to pet and calm Smoky as the car pulled up and George turned the motor off. Then she and Grandma watched as George helped Mama from the car . . . and they watched as George pulled Mama into his arms . . . and they watched as George kissed Mama—right on the mouth. And they watched, and giggled, as Mama looked at both of them with flushed cheeks and the biggest smile Lucy had ever seen.

Oh, yes! Lucy knew without the slightest shadow of doubt that this was the very best Christmas ever—the best Christmas in the whole wide world!

Melody Carlson is the author of more than two hundred books, including fiction, nonfiction, and gift books for adults, young adults, and children. She is also the author of *Three Days, The Gift of Christmas Present, The Christmas Bus, An Irish Christmas, All I Have to Give, The Christmas Dog, Christmas at Harrington's,* and *The Christmas Shoppe.* Her writing has won several awards, including a Gold Medallion for *King of the Stable* (Crossway, 1998) and a Romance Writers of America Rita Award for *Homeward* (Multnomah, 1997), and she was nominated for a *Romantic Times* Career Achievement Award in the inspirational market. She lives with her husband in Sisters, Oregon. Visit her website at www.melodycarlson.com.

Christmas is a time for miracles.

CHRISTMAS ROSES

AMANDA CABOT

Cozy up with this romantic and heartwarming tale of unexpected love.

Award-winning and popular author
Dan Walsh is back with another
Christmas story full of nostalgia and love.

A family crisis brings an estranged son home for the holidays,
where he rediscovers the true meaning of Christmas and family.